DESCEND

SOPHIA FLORENZA

iUniverse®

DESCEND

iUniverse books may be ordered through booksellers or by contacting:

iUniverse
1663 Liberty Drive
Bloomington, IN 47403
www.iuniverse.com
1-800-Authors (1-800-288-4677)

ISBN: 978-1-5320-9135-3 (sc)
ISBN: 978-1-5320-9136-0 (e)

Print information available on the last page.

iUniverse rev. date: 12/30/2019

PROLOGUE: THE DEVIL'S A DERANGED GAME SHOW HOST

"You ready to play, little girl?" the maniacal voice teases me from somewhere in the darkness. It echoes in the cavernous space around me, reverberating off stone walls I can only picture in my mind. For all I know I could be next to another Incubus, a sick creation of Lucifer's that is ready to suck my soul into the Void. *I don't have time for this shit!*

My anxiety is through the roof. I can hear my heart racing and my stomach feels like it's in my throat. It's not the voice that scares me, but the suffocating absence of light stealing my vision. It's too dark for my eyes to even adjust. There're no silhouettes or shadows. There is nothing but the sounds of my heartbeat and a disembodied voice. A voice that seems to come from nowhere and everywhere all at once. I grit my teeth and try to push down my rising anxiety. I will not let that faceless coward Lucifer have the pleasure of seeing my fear. "Bring it, asshole."

"You sure you want to play this game?" Lucifer mocks, his condescending amusement at my expense is all but oozing from his words. "You know what the stakes are if you lose."

My hands clench into fists without conscious choice to do so. I can feel the bite of my nails against my palms. The need to hit someone almost overwhelms me. *No, Lucifer would do.*

I am feeling impotent because the lack of a visible target only serves to fuel my anger. I do know what the stakes are if I play. My life, and Lucifer is not even affording me the dignity of seeing him; the person who threatens it. "Shut the fuck up and begin your game!"

Light floods a spacious room. The dazzling radiance is blinding me before I can determine my surroundings. I try to blink away the black spots, stealing my ability to focus, with no avail.

"Welcome to our game!" my tormentor's disembodied voice says in a tone that sounds like a game show host; but on LSD. "Please welcome our contestant…."

How did I end up here?!

Let's start from the beginning…

CHAPTER 1

OMENS

Back when I still had a sense of time, was a normal human girl, and nights were an actual thing. I'll start on Friday the 13th for those of you who still have the luxury of calendars

The hot water beats against my skin, cascading down my body, pushing away the aches of the day. My pale skin reddens at the water's temperature, but I relish the heat, like it's cleansing me of the mundane that was my day. You'd think that on your birthday, you wouldn't have to go to work and classes.

But unfortunately, adulting doesn't work that way. No matter what my life has thrown at me, though, I've always stood my ground and gave it the bird in return. I'd made it through a day of boring teachers and asking if people wanted paper or plastic, and my reward is this shower. My birthday is about to begin, and I'm not counting the rest of it. Despite my low key plans with friends, I can't help but feel a little excited because I'm finally twenty-one! Even though I've been drinking for years, now it's finally legal.

Turning off the water after rinsing the last of the shampoo out of my short pixie cut hair, I reach out past the shower curtain for a towel. Finding a towel, AKA bath sheet, on the shelving beside the shower, I pull the fluffy, navy blue bath sheet inside the shower with me. I've always found it weird that the big comfy towels are called bath sheets. I tend to think of them as body towels, and the regular towels were meant for hair when you're too lazy to get it cut. With my short locks, I don't need one of those. I dry my hair and body with the bath sheet, then wrap it around me, opening the shower curtain and stepping out.

The bathroom mirror is covered in steam from my shower. But I use a hand towel to wipe it away and am rewarded by the sight of my brown eyes blinking back at me. They sparkle with contentment, and I smile at my reflection.

Despite knowing I'll never be the sort of beauty that graces magazine covers, I actually like the way I look. I'm five foot four and shaped like an hourglass, more like Marilyn Monroe than Angelina Jolie. If I'd been born in the 50s, I would have been a sex symbol. Of course, if I had, I'd deal with even more mansplaining than I already do, so I'm okay with missing my body type's heyday. My spiky brown hair fits well with my personality, a lot of fight in a little package. I'm happy that I don't have boys lining up outside my door, because they're no prize either. Have you seen how the high school boys act these days? It's either an asshole, dickhead, or gay. The boys at the local state college I attend are no better.

They don't want relationships; they want a quick lay. The boys these days "supposedly" want to experience life before taking the plunge into commitment. I'm not going to waste my time becoming one of their experiences. So I'm virgin without a lot of guys noticing me because of my boob size, but not turned off by the short hair vibe. *I* like the way I look, and that's all that matters.

I brush my hair and teeth before exiting the en suite bathroom, dressed in my towel. Even though I'm in college I live with my parents; in the bedroom I grew up in. It may be a millennial thing to do, but it also gives me the chance to save my meager grocery store paycheck. I plan on getting a decent place after I graduate. Besides, I'm an adopted, only child, and my parents are in no more of a hurry to get rid of me than I am to leave.

As I exit the bathroom, I can't help but smile at the wall mural my mom painted for me when I was six. Even though my mom is a stay-at-home, she's also a talented artist who uses the walls of our house as her canvas. The walls of my suite are blue, my favorite color and the painting is opposite the door to my bathroom. The first thing I always see when I am getting ready for the day.

The picture is a play on my name, Seraphim, though I usually go by Sera. My name is one of the few gifts my biological parents left me with, and the fact that they chose it for me is the only thing I know about them. The illustration uses the wall's color as a background, and my mom added candy-like cotton clouds to make that section of the wall look like the sky. My name is etched into the fluffy white clouds so flawlessly it looks like an accent of the light. A warrior angel floats above the clouds, her large, light gray wings spread out behind her. She holds a gleaming silver sword above her head in her right hand, as if she's calling a waiting militia to arms. A beautiful silver shield adorns her right arm, and she is wearing a flowing white gown open at the front, revealing white pants. The angel is sporting white leather boots laced to her knees. Her long brown curls flow about her face, and my favorite part of the picture is that her face looks like mine. As if my mom could see the future and know exactly how I'd look in adulthood. Sure, she got the long curls wrong, but my mom's a lot more girly than I am, so a few misconceptions are to be expected.

I run my fingertips along the overflowing bookcase as I walk towards the closet to choose my outfit for the evening. Touching the books makes me feel warm inside because these books were my first friends. Before I met my current friends from high school, I spent most of my childhood alone and bullied. Being socially awkward made me an outcaste. Books offered me solace, an escape from my peers and more they gave me knowledge. I love to learn new things, ranging from science to history or get hooked reading a romantic adventure. I imagine meeting a man who could interest me, and he would want me for who I am in return. I'm starting to think that kind of man doesn't exist.

When I reach the closet, I pull out a tank top, blue jeans, a belt, and black military style boots. No need to impress anyone at Assisi's. Only the locals go there to hang out and have a few drinks. Besides, I'd rather be comfortable and happy than miserable and getting looks from men I have no interest in.

As I pull on my clothes, I glance at my computer. The screensaver tells me the date and the phases of the moon, something that's always been an interest to me. Today is Friday the 13th with a full blood moon. Creepy omens, but I chuckle to myself because I find the coincidence amusing. I'm not the type of person who believes in superstition, so the fact that both ominous signs are showing up on my birthday is a bit of a compliment.

Walking over to my vanity, I take a seat in front of it. I don't usually bother with makeup but tonight's my birthday, and I'm in the mood. Even now, though, I only plan to wear blush, eyeliner, eye shadow, and lip gloss. I inherited a flawless complexion; no need to cover it up with anything except sunblock.

I hear a knock on my bedroom door and glance up at the creaking sound of the door hinges moving.

"How's my birthday girl?" my mom asks as she enters the room. Her long blonde hair is swept back from her face in a regal French twist. Even though she unlikely hasn't left the house to do anything more than errands today. She's carrying a slinky dress covered in sequins on a hanger, and I bite back a sigh, unwilling to hurt her feelings. She's been attempting to place some frilly outfit onto my body since junior high. *Not happening!*

Pointing to the outfit, I politely tell her, "No thanks, mom. It's beautiful but definitely not for me."

She sighs in defeat, knowing that I'll never wear it, but inwardly I kind of have to applaud her tenacity. No matter how many times I reject her fashion suggestions, she always keeps coming back with new ones. My mom, Lilith, reminds me of Donna Reed; still wearing things that flatter her and that are considered stylish. Me? I stick to tank tops or T-shirts, jeans, and black heavy-soled boots. Fashion is not my thing.

Her blue eyes water as she looks over at the shelves of swimming trophies, medals, and ribbons on the opposite wall. "I remember when you won those. You were so small back then, the little fish who outswam all the bigger ones."

Before attending high school, I was in the city's community swim team until it was purchased by a for-profit gym and the free swimming programs closed for good. If I could afford it, I would join the gym so I could keep swimming for leisure. I find being in a pool, blocking the world out, and letting your mind drift the most peaceful feeling in the world. But my parents do enough for me, and I'm not going to ask them for a gym membership on top of all that they already do.

My mom's kind of an in the moment person, so her nostalgia alarms me. "Are you okay?" I ask, setting down my eyeliner pencil and giving her my full attention. She wipes away the tears that haven't quite fallen and pulls herself to her full five-foot-seven inch height, looking every inch the former high school prom queen that she once was. She shakes her head a bit as if to dislodge the somber mood. "I'm fine. I can't believe you're already twenty-one when it seems like yesterday you were my newborn baby girl."

You'd think with my mom's taller blonde stature I'd have realized as a kid that I was adopted. But my dad, Adam, shares my brown hair and eye color. Though he's taller than Mom, he hasn't broken six feet. Growing up, I always assumed I took after him. My parents have always treated me like their own, and I didn't even understand what adoption meant until Mom told me.

"You know that no matter how old I get, I'll always think you're the bestest mom in the world, right?" I tell her with a smile, intentionally using bad grammar to hopefully coax a smile in return.

She laughs, hanging the rejected outfit on the doorknob. She walks over to me, spinning me in my seat, so I face the mirror again. "Of course you will, because I am the bestest mom in the world. But you're going to look kinda funny if you leave this house with only half your eyeliner done, so you better do that."

I look up at her in the mirror, grateful to have her in my life. Not that I'd tell her that, because one compliment a night is enough. Picking up the pencil, I finish applying my makeup.

"So, birthday girl," she says as she toys with the ends of my hair. "I haven't seen you all day, and you never did tell me how you're doing."

"I'm good mom, getting ready for the girls to take me out," I reply.

"That sounds like fun…" Her voice drifting off and I can hear a warning coming on.

I rush on, "We're going to Assisi's to have a few drinks and hang out," I tell her before she can get to the "but" in that sentence. "Very low key, just the way I like it."

"Well," she sighs. "Be careful and don't accept open drinks from strangers, it's too easy for them to slip you a date rape drug."

I roll my eyes and turn from the mirror to look at my mom. I know that she wants me safe, but I think I got it. "I will be careful and won't drink too much, I promise."

She gives me a soft smile, but her eyes are filled with worry and sadness. I wonder if it's because she has finally realized I'm not her little girl anymore.

"Where's Dad? I thought he would be home by now to wish me a happy birthday?" I ask. My Dad's a prominent city lawyer, though I don't know what kind of law he practices. The cases must be significant, though, considering he's the only one bringing home a salary. He works a lot of hours because of his job, but he's proud of what he does, so a part of me can't blame him.

Mom frowns because she doesn't want to answer me. I've heard the usual excuses for when Dad's not coming. "You know how your father gets, Sera; this is a huge case for him, almost life-changing in a way."

I shrug my shoulders, hiding my disappointment —not the first time my dad has forgotten an important day. My father sometimes gets too involved in a case, forgetting to eat, sleep, or come home. I'm proud of his success, but days like today, when it's my birthday, and he's not here, it's hard to focus on that.

I hear a car horn and pocket my iPhone, my most expensive possession. I'm not materialistic by nature. Standing up from the vanity, I turn and, hug my mom. "Gotta go, Mary's here. I'll text you if we decide to go somewhere else after Assisi's."

"Okay. Have fun, be safe, and….good luck. We love you," my mom says while giving me a return hug.

I look at my mom in confusion, wondering why I need luck going to a bar. I hope to God that she isn't talking about me getting laid tonight. *Gross!*

Pretending that nothing my mom said was amiss, I reply, "Love you too, Mom. See ya later."

Should have thought something was weird about her telling me good luck. But I am excited about having my first legal drink and being with my friends.

CHAPTER 2

The Guide

Walking out of the house, down the porch steps, I see Beatrice and Rachael waving at me from the backseat of Mary's car. Mary's parents gave her their used silver Mercedes when she graduated from high school. The pristine condition of the car still makes it look new, and it's her pride and joy.

It's fortunate for me that Mary loves to chauffer us around because I don't own a car. Most places I need to go are only a few miles away, so I ride my bike. It saves me money on car-related expenses, and riding helps prevent me from growing into a rotund-like shape. I have curves, and I like to keep them in the right places instead of the wrong ones.

I open the front passenger door and slide into the black leather seat. "Hey, chicas!"

"Happy birthday, Sera!" my three friends scream in unison. I met my friends in high school, they were the first peers I'd met who appreciated my sense of humor and sarcasm. Labeled social outcasts, we were too intellectual and independent to be part of a nerd, art, or jock group. And weren't interested in the boys our high school had to offer. Girls with intelligence and wit to match are underappreciated in the sheltered world of a high school campus. We bonded over our shared isolation, and the four of us have been close ever since.

"Thanks, guys!" I reply, smiling as I buckle my seat belt.

"Your birthday chariot awaits, Ms. Dante," Mary says to me in a ridiculous tone. Her dimples accent her slightly chubby cheeks as she smiles and pretends to tip an invisible hat to me. "Where would you like to go?" she teases, knowing full well that there is only one place to go tonight.

I lean back in my seat, tapping a finger against my lips as I pretend to consider my destination options. We all knew in a city this small there weren't any, but it's always fun to pretend. "Hmmm, how about Assisi's?"

Mary's striking blue eyes twinkle as she says, "As you wish, Ms. Dante." She backs the car out of the driveway and turns down the street. My neighborhood has manicured lawns with cookie cutter two-story brick colonial houses. Like my own.

"How was your day, Mary?" I ask looking at her. Her dirty blonde hair is being pulled up in a ponytail, fitting with her features that can best be described as cute.

"Eh," she huffs, puffing her pale cheeks to blow out air in an extended sigh. "Working for tips sucks!" Mary works at the local diner, busting her ass every day to afford her college classes, car insurance, and gas. Her parents may have given her a Mercedes, but they're sticklers about her making her own way in the world. Fortunately, she's a go-getter by acing college like a pro. Despite working full-time, and trying to earn a graphics design scholarship from a prestigious art school. I don't know when the girl sleeps with how busy she is.

I turn to the other two girls in the backseat. "How about you, Beatrice? Almost done with that marketing project?"

Beatrice shrugs, her long, flat ironed black hair slides over her mocha colored shoulder as she moves. "Almost finished. I need to add a few more things," she replies with a bored look. Beatrice is anal retentive. Everything has to be perfect, or she goes nuts working herself into a frenzy until she vomits. Like mine, her parents are paying her tuition, so the only thing she has to focus on in her life is school. Sometimes I wonder if she'd be a little more chill about school if she had more to divide her attention.

"I'm sure it's already wonderful," I tell her in an attempt to prevent a full-on meltdown. We're always there for her when she goes into anal mode, assuring her she'll get an excellent grade. Like she always does, but it's part of being her friend. I don't mind doing that, but I only get one 21st birthday, and I don't want to spend it catering to her insecurities.

Her beautiful black eyes flash with anger as she scowls at me. "How would you even know without reading it, Sera? It's not right yet. I'll know when it's finished, and right now it's not finished!"

Not willing to argue on my birthday, I turn to Rachael. "So, Rache, are you still sane after watching toddlers run around all day?" Rachael works in a daycare and goes to school part-time to earn a teaching degree. With so many siblings, her family has always struggled with money and can't afford to pay for her tuition. Even if they wanted to.

She grins, her red hair in a ponytail swaying back and forth as she shakes her head,. "It's not as bad as you think, Sera," she says. "Each kid has their unique cuteness." Rachael has the patience of a saint. Those kids could be, and most likely are, little monsters, and she'd still adores them.

I chuckle. "I'll take your word for it."

"You say that," she says with a smile that lights up her freckled face, "but there's nothing in the world like seeing a little kid smile or when they hug you."

"You mean with their sticky hands and dirty bodies?" I quip.

She rolls her calm, blue eyes at my response. "Someday you'll love kids as much as I do, and then I'm going to tell you I told you so."

"I wouldn't hold your breath," I tell her. "Kids are not on the agenda, today or any day in my future."

Rachel gives me one of those knowing smiles that says without words that she knows something I don't. I know what she's thinking. Having grown up in a big family, she's always wanted the same for herself, despite the money issues that having a big family has caused.

She can't imagine anyone not wanting children, but I'm not sure I do. Some people aren't made to be parents, and I believe I'm one of them. Maybe she's right, and I'll change my mind someday, but right now I can't imagine that I would. Even if on the off chance I managed to have a kid that wasn't a complete monster because I chose not to have a career and would home school instead. I would not subject my child to the same sort of monsters I met in school. Considering how miserable school was until I met the three of them, I can't imagine doing that to another person I cared about. So, no, I don't think kids will ever be for me.

"So, Sera," Mary said cutting into my disturbing thoughts of parenthood. "How was work?"

"Boring," I reply without much thought. I work as a cashier at the local pharmacy. It's one of those more prominent places where they think of themselves as more than a drug store, but a one-stop shop. Where you can get all your needs while picking up your prescriptions. Except, what they don't tell the customers is that everything outside of the meds is jacked up in price and they'd be better off making two stops. I work at the front counter checking out the people that fall for the idea of convenience and shopping like a regular store. The customers are usually senior citizens. Nothing is challenging about my job, but it's a paycheck. The hardest part of my work is biting my tongue and not telling the customers they can get the same things for half the price a block over at the grocery store.

"Meet any guys?" Rachel asks

"All the time," I say sarcastically. "But I wouldn't consider free senior citizen meals at the local rotary club a date."

"Sera, you're too picky," Beatrice interjects. That's rich coming from her. While my friends a do go on dates, I've never met anyone pickier than Bea.

"So, what you're telling me is that you think I ought to go to the retirement center the next time I'm asked to lunch?" I joke.

"Well, yeah," Mary says. "If he's rich and about to kick the bucket, I can't think of a better marriage candidate."

We all laugh because everyone knows Mary isn't serious. She may joke about being cutthroat and hardcore, but she wouldn't be someone I wanted to be around if she actually was that way.

As we get closer to Assisi's, our conversations stop and a heavy silence fills the car, making the drive weird and uncomfortable. I can't think of a reason that everyone would be so lost in their thoughts on the way to my girls' night out birthday bash.

"So, who's buying my first legal drink tonight?" I ask to break the strange silence. When no one replies, I look at my companions. Mary's eyes are glued to the road, and both girls in the back are looking out their windows.

I was about to ask again, to try and pull them from whatever dark thoughts had stolen their attention, when Mary cries, "We're here!" turning the car into Assisi's parking lot.

After Mary parks, all four of us get out of the car and start walking to the front door. Assisi's is a small bar with nice wooden siding wrapped around the building. Everything is well maintained with no garbage in the well-lit parking lot, giving the bar a welcoming ambiance.

Walking into Assisi's is nothing new. My friends and I have hung out here playing pool since we all turned eighteen. It is your typical local bar, with regular customers sitting in their designated seats. I guess we are kind of regulars ourselves, but I'd never thought of us as such because I couldn't legally drink there before now. That's not to say I'd never had a drink in Assisi's, because the owner, Frank, was nice about turning his head if someone else bought your drinks. So long as you didn't try to buy them yourself. Frank, who is somewhere between his upper thirties to mid-forties, is surprisingly cool for his age.

The bar's interior reflects the exterior, both clean and well kept, the inside feeling a bit like coming home. The walls and furniture are a combination of mahogany wood and dark brown leather with pictures of Italy adorning each wall. A three-sided bar huggs the back wall with a big screen TV playing a sporting event behind it. High and regular tables are placed in an orderly fashion around the bar, and pool tables line the opposite wall. I knew without checking that if I went to play a game, the sticks would be straight with no wear at the tips. Frank would never allow anything less. Finding everything inside in pristine condition is as routine as finding Frank behind the bar dressed in his usual brown slacks and matching shirt.

Seeing us walk in, Frank looks up and smiles, accenting the little laugh lines at the edges of his soft gray eyes. "Here's the birthday girl! What do you want for your first drink tonight?"

Before I can answer, a deep, male voice speaks from the far end of the bar. "She'll start with a Holy Fire shot tonight. On me."

Frank stops moving and turns towards the owner of the voice, the light from the overhead sconces highlighting his golden skin. The proof of a man who loves to be outside. But Frank suddenly goes slightly pale, and his always present smile disappears as he nods his head in agreement. "Good choice."

I turn my head, looking down the bar, trying to see who bought me my first drink. I'm a little alarmed at the sadness tinting Frank's usual pleasant voice and observing his reluctant reaction to the stranger's order. Who could make Frank react that way, and do I even want him to buy me a drink? At the same time, I wonder why my friends aren't say anything. Wasn't the whole point in them taking me out tonight that they be the ones who buy the first round?

From where I stand, I'm too short to see who made the request at the end of the bar, so I look back at Frank for a sign on whether I should explore further. The strange encounter seems to have occupied Frank's mind as he focuses on fixing the drink. The yellow overhead lighting behind the bar reflects off his full head of brown hair, sparkling on the few strands of gray. Since Frank seems busy in making my first legal drink, I decide to return to searching for the stranger.

My friends murmur something behind me about finding a table, but I'm more concerned with moving closer to the bar so I can see the owner of that voice. My eyes land on an alluring paragon of a man sitting at the end of the bar, even his nose is perfect. His full, extremely kissable looking lips slide into a grin as he notices my gaze.

As I meet the stranger's eyes, and I feel like time is standing still, and everything around us disappears. At this moment there's only him and me. Heat infuses every molecule of my skin, sending feelings of desire through my body. I lick my lips, wondering what he would taste like if I were kissed by him. I feel wet with need, from a single look and the feeling scares me. I've never been attracted to anyone before, and certainly not in a manner that's so all-encompassing and almost violent in nature.

I used to wonder if something was wrong with me because of my lack of interest in the men I meet. Now that I am, for the first time, actually attracted to someone, I am entirely out of my element. It can't be normal to feel like this, so out of control of your own body, the first time you look at someone.

When the Adonis rises from his stool and approaches, I break his gaze, searching for my friends like they are a lifeline. My friends would help me feel confident with meeting this stranger and not feel uncertain. Looking behind me, I find them sitting at the corner table against the far wall, watching me. Frowning, I give them a "what the fuck" look. What kind of friends abandon you when you need obvious saving? Okay, it might not have been clear to them, when they're always after me to start dating, but it's a big flashing neon sign to me. I'm not ready to talk to this stranger without one of them beside me. Holding my hand, if I want to be truly honest. And if they're going to be really nice, doing most of the talking for me. I'm not equipped to converse with men who look like him.

My friends smile and wave back at me, but no one makes a move to come to my rescue. They seem content, even entertained, by the idea of watching me drown, or making a complete fool of myself. Realizing I'll get no help from that corner, I turn back. My gaze connects with a muscular chest covered by a button down grey dress shirt, too close to my face.

Startled, I take a step back, slowly moving my gaze from his chest to his face. The stranger is at least six foot one with a firm, lean runner's build I all but ache to run my hands over. He stands only inches away from me, with his hands tucked into the pockets of his black dress slacks.

I clench my fists to prevent myself from doing something more stupid, like acting on my impulses. It's bad enough that all I seem capable of doing is standing here gaping at him like a fish out of water.

I honestly didn't believe men this attractive existed outside of photo-shopped magazines and digitally altered cinema. Confronted with a real-life specimen of such perfection, I seem to have forgotten how to speak, I'm lucky I can even remember to breathe.

He looks down at me, with grey eyes fringed with dark lashes, waiting until I collect myself enough to meet his gaze. "What's your name?" he asks in a calming tone.

Though his tone is relaxing, I still can't seem to find my voice. I stare at him dumbfounded, bombarded by the thoughts in my head. *He's got to think I'm a simpleton who doesn't even know her own name. This is ridiculous; of course, I know my own name. It's Sera, come on mouth, work, you can do it, say "Sera". I cannot stand here acting like recalling my own name is some kind of riddle.*

The stranger pulls his large hand from his pocket, reaching over to rest it lightly on my shoulder. A feeling of serenity washes over me as his hand slides from my shoulder down my arm, before returning to his pocket as if he'd never touched me at all.

"Seraphim," I finally say with newfound calm. "Sera for short."

The soft, golden highlights in his almost military-cut, dark brown hair seem to gleam in the dim lighting of the room as he leans against the bar. "Seraphim, hmmm...I like that."

He continues to stare at me as if waiting for me to reply, but even if I am calmer than I'd been at the beginning, I can't think of a single thing to say. I glance down at the bar making the grains of wood seem like it is the most exciting thing I've ever seen, morbidly embarrassed at my lack of conversational skills.

"My name is Virgil by the way."

My head snaps up, and I reach out my right hand to perform a proper handshake. Yep, that's what I should have been doing in that long awkward pause, asking his name. "Nice to meet you, Virgil."

Smiling, he grabs my outstretched hand. His hand is warm and soft. I like how my hand fits perfectly in his. Reluctantly I let go, but only because the handshake lasts a bit too long to be considered normal.

It's as I release his hand that I'm struck with an epiphany. The situation, from the male model in front of me to the fact that my friends abandoned me, finally makes sense. *Did they buy me an escort?* I flush with embarrassment, remembering that no guy has ever been attracted to me like this before. Sure I got the obnoxious "prove that you're not a lesbian" challenges, not even worth acknowledging. But I don't consider those genuine interests. No man has ever bought me or drink or anything for that matter except my dad. No reality exists where a guy that looks like Virgil notices me unless he's being paid to do so.

"Drink is ready Sera," Frank says, pulling me out of my own head.

I turn to give Frank my cash because I didn't want a paid service date. It's humiliating enough to know I could never land a handsome guy like the one in front of me, I can't stomach the thought of his buying my drinks too. I can't even bring myself to look at him anymore. I'm torn between mortification and indignation. *How could my closest friends ever think I'd be okay with the idea of them hiring me an escort? Don't they know me at all? Do they think I'm that much of a loser?!*

"I said the drink was on me," Virgil says with evident irritation, placing his hand over mine to stop me from paying Frank. With his other hand, he hands Frank a credit card.

Ignoring my evident displeasure, Frank takes the card and runs it.

I yank my hand away and look up at him. "Listen, I know what my friends did, and I don't need a paid escort to land a date. Thanks for offering to pay for my first legal drink, but I'd rather get my own date." I push some cash into his hand and grab the shot from the bar. "Here's the money for the drink. No harm, no foul."

Pivoting on my heel with every intention of walking to the table and me telling my so-called friends, what I think of their cruel birthday gift, I glance down at the glass in my hand. I pause, fascinated by the shot's unique color. The drink looks like glowing liquid fire, and the glass is almost warm to the touch. It seems to dance the same way an actual fire would. I've never seen anything like it before. Shaking my head to free my concentration, I remind myself that I have more pressing matters than staring at an eccentric beverage.

I look back at the table where the traitors I used to call friends are still sitting. Unlike before, all conversation between them has ceased, and they stare back at me in silence. It's likely they can see my unhappiness from here. I vaguely think of how embarrassing it'll be to call my mom to pick me up and where I'll find the words to explain to her what has happened, but I shrug that off too. It's a problem for later. As I start to walk away, preparing to officially end my friendships I'm stopped by a firm hand on my shoulder.

"I'm not a paid escort," Virgil announces loud enough that all other conversation in the establishment seems to stop and the patrons turn to stare at us. "I saw something that I liked and wanted to show my appreciation."

I turn back to him with my jaw hanging and heat rushing to my cheeks. If my incorrect assumptions weren't embarrassing enough, the fact that everyone else in the bar knows what I fool I am makes me wish the ground would open and swallow me whole. "Oh!" I stammer quietly in hopes our audience won't overhear, "I'm sorry. It's that, well, someone that looks like you has never given me a second look before." I look down to study the tips of my black boots, silently wishing I could disappear. *The first time a guy actually notices me and I act like a complete ass. Why is this my life?*

He slips a hand beneath my chin, tipping up my face upward to meet his gaze. "The men you've been meeting are fools." *What do I even say to that?* I stare at him awestruck as a response fails to come to mind.

Virgil tilts his head nodding at the shot still in my left hand. "Well, drink up, birthday girl."

With no words to return, I follow his direction and take the shot. It burns like fire down my throat, through my body, making me cough and gasp for air. Don't get me wrong. I've had shots, but none that stole my breath like this. As my breath returns, I feel euphoric, weightless and grounded at the same time. I'm struck with a sensation of awareness, as if my senses have heightened beyond what they've ever been.

Looking up into Virgil's eyes, I notice that his grey eyes are now swirling, like a fucking storm at sea. *What the hell?* I look away, unable to deal with the almost hypnotic movement of his eyes. It's then I notice that we're all but alone in the once crowded establishment. Everyone is gone except Virgil, Frank, my friends, and me. Even the few familiar faces that remain look like something out of a cartoon. My friends are surrounded by halos of golden light. Frank looks like a monk straight out of the classic Robin Hood movie with Errol Flynn. He even has the strange half bald hair cut and a brown habit.

"Where did everyone go?" I murmur, half to myself. I turn back to Virgil. "What the fuck did you give me? Did you put a hallucinogen in my drink?"

"They're still here, but on another plane of existence. I didn't think they needed to witness your awakening," Virgil answers. "Seraphim, we need you to come with me."

"We?" I ask, refusing to even question what in the bloody hell an awakening was or how people could suddenly be on another plane of existence. I can't even acknowledge his crazy behavior. It would be like encouraging the lunatic. There is a tap on my shoulder. My three friends stand there, still glowing like deranged human light bulbs. "What the fuck is going on? Why is Frank wearing a monk's habit? And how the hell did he get his hair to look like a Franciscan monk?" I ask.

"I put on a glamour to hide my true appearance," Frank answers, drawing my attention toward him.

"What?" I ask, knowing that there is an expression of panic etched all over my face.

Frank sighs. " I am Saint Francis of Assisi," he states as if telling me he's a saint who died almost 800 years ago was the most normal thing in the world.

"Joan of Arc," I quip, "pleased to meet you." What can I say? Sarcasm is my go-to defense mechanism. "Wait, what the fuck was in that drink and what is a 'glamour'?"

Frank looks at me patiently, seeming sympathetic to my confusion. "That shot was pure Holy Fire, a watered-down version of the same substance that brought destruction to the cities of Sodom and Gomorrah when the Creator made it rain down on them. Now, you can see the world that was hidden to you. You can see past the glamours, our costumes that conceal us from the mortal world. You can now recognize the angels and demons that walk the world of man."

"Ahhh. That explains everything!" I respond in a tone that's equal parts sarcasm and panic. My mind jumps to the only logical conclusion.

"When can I wake up from this freaky-ass dream?" *I don't remember laying down for a nap.*

"Seraphim," Mary's voice interrupts my thoughts, and I turn to my three fake friends. "We are sorry to deceive you like this, but you have to go with Virgil, now, tonight."

"Why?" I ask. "What the fuck is going on?!" My panicked feelings have escalated to agitation and fear. *Did the room get smaller? Why does it feel like all the air is draining out of here without any left for me?*

"I will explain on the way to The Inferno," Virgil states, the sound of his voice pulling me from my impending panic attack.

Now I'm genuinely perplexed. "The Inferno? That posh underground nightclub that's impossible for someone like me to get into?"

"The same," Virgil answers.

"I'm not dressed to go to some nightclub." I glance down at myself, knowing it's more of an excuse to get the fuck away from these people than a real reason not to go.

"No worries, you'll get in wearing that," Virgil explains as if everything's settled.

"Um, I'm still not going because I don't know who the fuck you are." I turn to my so-called friends. "And I don't know who you three bitches are either. I'm leaving."

"Sera, please!" Beatrice intones. "We're your friends, and we care about you. But we're also here to protect you while there is a need for you. You are now needed and must go with Virgil. Please? It's imperative that you go!"

"No!" I snapped, fed up with this nightmare. "I'm not going to some club with a random stranger who put some hallucinogen in my drink. I'm going to call an Uber and go home!"

"Why the fuck do I get stuck with this bullshit?" Virgil sighs.

I turn to leave, refusing to even acknowledge his complaint that I'm some kind of a chore for him. "Give me a second, and I won't be a bother at all, because I won't be here at all." Feeling a zap against my skin and then I don't feel or see anything at all.

CHAPTER 3

THE INFERNO

Okay, so getting zapped and blacking out was not on my to-do birthday list. But waking up in the back seat of an SUV, feeling like my head got bashed in by a sledgehammer, pisses me the fuck-off. I'm on my back, and I turn my head to the driver.

My fucking zapper/kidnapper is driving us to god knows where. "What the fuck happened and where the fuck are we going?!" I yell.

"My, my, that's a lot of fucks in one sentence. Care for a vowel?" Virgil says with dripping sarcasm, not bothering to turn his head.

"Suck a cock" I retort. I start sitting up — big mistake.

Whatever Virgil zapped me with did a number on my head, making me feel woozy. "Better not barf on my leather upholstery." Him saying that almost makes me want to puke all over his expensive SUV. Almost.

Instead, I lay back down because I hate puking more than anything. "It'll wear off." I flip him the bird. I start feeling around my pockets, looking for my phone. *Shit! My phone and bank card are gone. Definitely up the creek!*

"So" Virgil continues, "because you are currently not in the mood to speak, this will give me an opportunity to explain the situation." I stay silent waiting for him to go on. "You were chosen to save seven angels and one pure soul from Limbo and Hell." He keeps speaking.

"The Creator and Lucifer made a bet. Lucifer lost. And because he's Lucifer, he's currently a sore loser, acting like a child. The Creator is now forced to send someone to Hell to retrieve his winnings. He chose you. Any questions?" Knowing I was still feeling like shit, I couldn't answer. "No? Nothing? Good." *Handsome motherfucker is getting cock punched first chance I get!*

Virgil keeps on driving for quite a while. The throbbing and nausea ebb away to where I am finally able to sit up. "That was a fast recovery," Virgil says into the rearview mirror. I heard a hint of surprise in his voice.

"Always was a fast healer," I reply. "What the fuck did you zap me with anyway?" I ask.

"As your guide, I was imbued with some heavenly powers. Knocking people unconscious is one of them," is the response. I roll my eyes.

"Why did The Creator choose me?" I ask. Virgil shrugs his shoulders.

"No fucking clue. Was told to guide you and that's it." I loudly huff my annoyance that I'm forced to sit here and listen to this crap.

"I want my phone back so I can call my mom!" I demand.

"Not until we get to our first stop," Virgil says.

"Where are we going?" I demand.

"I told you, The Inferno," states Virgil.

"Why are we going to a nightclub if I'm supposed to be going to Hell?" I see Virgil is clenching his jaw and tightening his hands on the steering wheel.

"Okay," I say, going into my sarcastic, patronizing mode. "Let us pretend I don't know anything about going to Hell to save angels and souls. Or even knowing how I would get to Hell without dying. Plus I don't believe the psychotic bullshit story you just told me. I am not going to fight you because I want to get my phone back and call my mom. So please help me the fuck out or go to Hell yourself." I say with as much sarcasm and wit I can muster while folding my arms across my chest.

I hear Virgil huff in exasperation. "The Inferno is a front. A doorway to Hell is located there. Only the unbelieving or most wicked are allowed in. That's why it's a posh nightclub."

"I'm guessing that most of these lost souls are rich?" I ask.

Virgil nods, "And powerful," he remarks.

I keep silent for the rest of the drive.

A few minutes later we are pulling up to a big brick building with a faint glowing marquee with "The Inferno" on it. There is a very long line wrapping around the building. I see a lot of scantily dressed young girls. Dressed to the nines waiting to get in or trying to get the attention of the groups of dressed up men pulling up to the valet in expensive cars; automatically let in by the enormous bouncers keeping crowd control.

"Oh look, I forgot to put on my slut wear tonight. Guess we will have to come back another time," I comment dryly.

"Nice try," Virgil says as he's pulling up to the valet. *I'm in no mood for this shit.*

The young male valet opens my door then walks around to open Virgil's door. Sliding out of the SUV, standing on the red carpet leading into the club, I hear a few snickers from the girls in the front of the line. "Like they would let dikes like her in" one comments.

"Yeah, no guy or girl would want to touch that," another girl says while the group is laughing. I look down, wishing the ground could swallow me up. As I said, I'm in no mood for this shit.

I suddenly feel a finger under my chin, raising my head and soft lips on mine. Surprised, I jolt my head back in reflex but the moment was over. I look up at Virgil, and he takes my hand, leading me straight into the club.

As I'm walking past the line, I glance over at the judgmental bitches. They are staring at me in shock because Virgil is fucking hot and I'm being let in, dressed in jeans. I smile my 'fuck you' smile at the girls as I am walking past them.

I take a deep breath when the doors open for us, and we step into a dark corridor.

"Thank you," I tell Virgil, but he drops my hand and keeps walking down the corridor. For me get my phone to contact my parents and the police, there is nothing else I can do but follow him.

I can feel the beat of the music pounding through the floor and walls. Virgil stops at the end of the corridor, in front of a closed red door with a sign hanging from it that says "Limbo."

Waiting until I get close to him, Virgil commands, "Stay right behind me. We need to make a few stops before going through the gate. Oh, and do not stop and stare at the things you see. It could mean your death if you do." *Awesome!*

I don't say anything, nodding my head in understanding and clench my jaws. I always take the bad with the good, praying that this is a nightmare and will soon wake up.

"Here we go," mutters Virgil and opens the door. He walks through, and I'm right behind him; trying to stay close to him without touching him. I can feel his body heat which helps when I start looking around, noting the club ambiance with the strobe lights flashing in sync with the dark techno club mix blaring through the speakers — the base of the music vibrating the room, pounding all the way to my soul.

A considerable bar located on the side, stocked with every liquor imaginable. The bartenders are tossing bottles while making drinks, entertaining the guests. There is a second story industrial balcony that wraps around the entire club. And there is a mass of bodies on the dance floor, all moving with the music.

I see humans, monsters, and what looks like angels grinding against each other. The monsters are so fucking hideous that I'm wondering why the human men and women are dancing with them. The angels are on the other side of the physical spectrum; so fucking beautiful I want to cry.

Heeding Virgil's warning, I stop staring and turn my head to look straight into his back. I've seen enough weird shit in that thirty-second glance than I have wanted to see in a lifetime.

Virgil is fighting through the sea of gyrating bodies, pushing towards the set of stairs leading up to the balcony. Probably the VIP section. The stairs are roped off and guarded by two fugly orcish things, looking like they stepped out of a Tolkien book; but wearing suits. I don't know what Virgil says to them because of the loud music, but we are allowed up the stairs.

We climb up the stairs and turn right, passing sheer white curtains, which I am guessing are the VIP rooms. Even though I can't hear anything, my eyesight is working fine. From what I can tell from the moving silhouettes on the curtains, it looks like there is a lot of group sex happening. I keep my head and eyes forward and follow Virgil, ignoring the silhouettes. I'm no prude, but I'm not a voyeur either.

We walk to a red door at the end of the balcony, and without knocking, Virgil steps through with me tailing him. The door closes behind me, the music not invading the quietness of this room. It takes my ears a second to stop ringing.

We are in a dimly lit room, furnished like a CEO's office with plush black leather seats and a substantial black desk. Bookshelves lining the blood red painted walls. A faint light in the corner catches my attention.

I turn my head to get a better look at the light source, and I see a sword stuck in a stone, glowing. *Holy shit!* I've read so many fictional books and stories on the Arthurian tale, but I never dreamed about them. 'This is a weird dream' is my new mantra so I can deal with this fucked up situation.

"So, Virgil, what are you doing here with this little boy? You know boys are not my thing," a deep male voice grumbles. *What the fuck did he just say?* I step around Virgil and see a big man with glowing green eyes staring at me. I cannot see his face because of how dark the room is but the sound of his voice is making me wet. Probably another male model. But that does not give him the right to be an asshole.

I take a step forward towards the desk, all thoughts of caution thrown out. "Listen dick. I was out with my friends to celebrate my birthday when this butt plug," flicking a thumb towards Virgil "knocked me out, kidnapped me, and told me that I had to waltz into Hell to collect a bet between The Creator and Lucifer. I guess your balls were not big enough for The Creator to pick, so he chose a female instead. Am I missing anything?"

I hear Virgil snorting, trying not to laugh, and I see a little amusement dancing in my host's glowing green eyes. "She has some spunk. Good to know," he says to no one in particular, eyes still on me. "But if you wanted to see my balls little girl, all you have to do is ask. I got the biggest set between both realms." I do an inward eye roll. *As if.* He then stands up and walks around his desk, any light that the room has lands on his face. *I hate being right! Fucker is gorgeous!*

And he's got wings?!

He's either an angel or demon because his wings are leathery looking instead of the feathers I saw downstairs on the angels. "Who or what are you?" I ask as he steps under one of the lights.

Not only is he drop dead gorgeous, but his body is huge! I note that he's dressed in a suit and tie, has raven black hair, and black leather wings. Of course, he's sculpted like a Roman god. The very face of perfection. My nipples are hard and I'm soaking wet.

"I'm known as the patron saint of soldiers and was one of The Creator's generals, before the Fall," he states matter of factly. I know I am well versed in my theology and as I said before, I read a lot of fucking books.

"So you're both the Archangel Gabriel and the Patron Saint George? As in George, the dragon slayer?" I asked.

"Very good. You may call me G."

He takes a few steps closer to me until I finally realize how massive this guy is. I'm only five foot four, but this guy easily towers me at six foot four. And he's built like a warrior from the medieval ages. His arms could be the size of tree trunks.

G stares at me, studying me. I roll my eyes at him. "What?" I demand.

"You're much smaller and plainer than I've imagined," he states. *Ouch!*

"Well, you're much dumber than I've imagined, seeing you're here and not in Heaven. Do something to piss off your Creator?" I retort.

Virgil groans, loudly and whispers "Shit" and before I know it, G is using his size and starts marching at me; forcing me to back away from him. When I hit the wall, G is blocking me in with his body and his tree trunk arms are suddenly on either side of my head. "I will not tolerate any disrespect from anyone, even if The Creator chooses them.

You mention anything about Heaven and me again; I will break your fucking neck and burn your body to ensure no revival on the third day. You understand?"

All I could do is nod, and he drops his arms, stalking away. When I am able to find my voice, "Did you reference me coming back to life like Jesus Christ? No fucking way this is happening." I croak. This situation is becoming too surreal.

"I hope this a joke and not the chosen one," G says to Virgil, voice filled with disdain.

"Only one way to truly know," Virgil replies. They both turn to look at me. *Oh no!*

"See Excalibur over there?" G points to the sword in the stone.

"Let me guess," I interrupt, "like Arthur, I have to pull it out. Will I get to be King of England too and have Merlin as my magician?" I ask with dripping sarcasm.

"No," G says, "but if you can pull out Excalibur, you won't die, making you The Creator's chosen for this mission." The way he looks at me, he hopes that it is the former and not the latter.

"What if I refuse?" I ask.

"Then I will kill you. The end," replies G. *Dick!*

Knowing I have nowhere to go and can't escape through the only door that we came through, I grudgingly trudge to the glowing sword. For some reason, I feel drawn to it the closer I get, and then I can hear a soft hum. When I'm next to the hilt, the sword glows brighter, making me want to touch it. 'Touch me' I hear in my head. *Now I'm hearing voices!*

I touch the golden hilt, and something awakens inside me. Something that was empty but now filling me. 'You will be the greatest champion with me at your side' the voice says. 'Here is the power that was denied you your whole life,' and with that, raw, powerful energy starts ripping through me.

I feel like it's too much, and that I will shatter into a million pieces. 'Relax' the voice says. 'Don't fight what is rightfully yours.' I listen to the voice and start to hum the same tune.

'Now free me' says the voice. I pull the sword from the stone until it's all unsheathed. A bright light flashes, blinding me instantly and then I find myself falling towards darkness; feeling like something sucked the life out of me. 'Rest now, little one,' the voice says in my head. 'We have a long journey ahead of us.' And that is the last thing I remember.

CHAPTER 4

LIMBO

I hear a voice in my head. "Wake up, little one." I open my eyes and find myself staring up at the ceiling. The second time I've passed out today in a matter of hours. *I'm on a roll!*

Sitting up, I look around at my surroundings, finding myself on a nice leather couch in G's office. A sense of panic and dread starts to fill me. *Not a dream! I need to escape now!* I start looking around to see if Virgil and G are in the room. *Nope, all clear. Now for a weapon.*

"What do you want to do?". That voice. I turn my head around, looking for the source. "Who's there?" I ask the room.

"Down here, little one." I look down to my right, and there is the glowing sword, laying right next to me. *Holy Shit! A sword is speaking to me in my head. My parents are definitely going to institutionalize me once I wake up from this dream.*

"I can hear your thoughts and feel your emotions, little one. I know that you are scared right now and worried about your parents. But please try to refrain from blaspheming. I am a holy sword you know?"

Uh? Riiiight?

"Sorry, but you got the wrong person. I want to go home," I say in my head.

"I don't make mistakes, little one. You were born to do this task. And do not worry about your parents. They knew since the day that you were given to them that you were fated to take this journey."

What the fuck?

"My parents knew and didn't bother to warn me about this?!" I scream at the sword. There is no response. My chest starts to hurt, and feeling of remorse washes over me because of my parents' betrayal. No wonder I'm such a freak. Pulling my knees up into my chest, I lay my forehead onto my knees. "Not going to cry, not going to cry," I whisper to myself over and over again.

"Ahem." I look up, and there's G looking like a model with glowing green eyes but no wings, and standing next to him is Virgil. Also fucking beautiful. But looking closer at Virgil, I notice that his eyes are glowing dark silver.

Okay, whatever.

I try to focus and ignore the heat rushing down my thighs, caused by the attraction when I am looking at both men. Untangling my legs, I stand up, waiting for one of them to start talking.

I still can't forget the small kiss Virgil gave me before walking into the club. A pity kiss, no doubt because of what those stuck up bitches were saying about me.

Both men are now staring at me. There is a look of wonder on their faces. "What? Did I sprout another head or something?"

It is Virgil who comments, "Your eyes. They've changed."

I frown and start looking around for a mirror in G's office. "Here," the sword says "this will help." I look down, and the sword stops glowing, morphing the surface into a shiny mirror. I lift the sword to eye level and gasp. My eyes are not brown anymore! They are the lightest blue I have ever seen. Almost white. As if glowing like a dwarf star. *Oh my God!*

"What's happening to me?! What the fuck does this mean?!" I yell at both men. G crosses his massive arms, looking more than pissed that I have survived pulling the sword out of the stone and changing.

"What do you know of Archangels?" Virgil asks me.

Trying to remain calm, I shrug my shoulders. "Nothing but the mythology and biblical stories that mention them. Why?"

"During the Fall, The Creator sent the seven Archangels to battle Lucifer's demonic army. They are Gabriel, Uriel, Raphael, Barachiel, Jegudiel, Selaphiel, and Michael. They never returned to heaven. Instead, they were somehow corrupted and now are somewhere in the nine circles of Hell. Our task is to bring them home." Virgil is completely serious.

"Uh, if they were 'corrupted' as you say, aren't they now considered evil and should stay where they are?" I ask. And then I look at G, remembering that one of his names is Gabriel. And from his expression, I pissed him off even more. I look down at my hands and mutter, "Sorry."

"Only you have the power to remove the corruption. You will finally be releasing them back to heaven," Virgil explains.

"How the fuck do you propose I do I do that?" I snap.

"Leave me with her," G growls. *Oh shit.* Virgil complies, going through the red door and closing it behind him. I swallow hard. My heart is beating so fast and loud from my trepidation of being alone with him, that I'm sure G can hear it. I push down my anxiety and fear, not wanting to give G any more reason to feel that he has dominance over me.

I look G over. He changed into a tight, black T-shirt that doesn't hide his ripped chest and abs, and black military-style cargo pants complete with black combat boots. My mouth goes dry, and I get wet below. *God, he's gorgeous.*

He starts stalking towards me. "Listen, little girl. I know that you're more than inadequate for this job, but you survived pulling the sword out. So, stop your fucking whining and act like the boy you are trying to be, dressed like that with that haircut."

What did he just say to me?!

Now I'm beyond fucking pissed and stand my ground. "How about this, little boy" I scoff. "Go get bent and suck a bag of dicks. I love that

I'm stereotyped as a lesbian because I got short hair and don't wear Barbie clothes."

And then I step up to him and stick my pointer finger in his chest, poking him and staring into his eyes. "FYI, I like men. But I would never fuck you if you were the last man in this Goddamn universe. Got it, asshole?" I ask, putting as much venom in my voice as I can.

He's staring at me with those beautiful green eyes, and I'm looking up at his mouth. I want to kiss that mouth. Badly. I become aware that there is a heavy sexual tension in the room, and I start moving away from G. Before I could walk away further, I'm in G's arms. His mouth possessing mine.

I got my first kiss with Virgil and now my first make-out session with G. Happy birthday to me! And wow, what a kisser! He teases my lips and teeth open with his tongue, and I can feel a spark deep within me when our tongues collided.

With his body, G starts backing me up until the couch hits me in the back of the knees. He gently pushes me back, causing me to lay down with him on top of me; adjusting his weight so as not to crush me.

His hand is exploring my body. Rubbing his right hand down the side of my body and back up. Going underneath my tank top to rest on my belly. I'm filled with need, not sure where I want him touching me most.

He puts his knee between my legs to spread them apart so he can cradle his body there. Good thing I'm wearing jeans. Not giving my virginity to this asshole, even though he makes me feel so good right now.

I feel his hardness between my legs, through my jeans. *He's big!* Our tongues are still dancing and entwining, and my need is growing. I lift my hips to rub my jean zipper against his bulge and to hit the spot on my pussy that's throbbing. Like I said. Not a prude.

I hear him groan in the back of his throat. His hand goes under my shirt and wanders up to my breast, still cupped in a bra. He goes underneath the bra and starts kneading my flesh. Zing! A fire goes straight to the junction between my legs, making me wetter and hotter. My body is on fire, the pleasure intense, making me moan in kind.

He immediately breaks the kiss, removing his hand and body from me. The instant removal of G's body heat is like a cold blast from a refrigerator. G stands up, gives me a look of pure disdain, and walks to the red door. What the fuck happened?

Before opening the door, he turns to me and says, "You're very experienced with men, or you would have never been able to seduce me like that. But I would never be attracted to you unless you were using your energy. Don't ever use your energy on me again," he snarls as he opens the door and stomps out.

Ouch! The fuck?

That was a bucket of cold water to snap me out of my lust-filled haze. I get off the couch, straightening myself, burying G's rejection deep down so it would never hurt me. I've gotten plenty of practice from all the bullying I suffered through adolescence.

I clear my thoughts and steady my emotions so the sword can't hear me. I pick up the sword. "I'm going to call you Cal" I think to the sword.

"Cal….hmmm? I like it" the sword responds in my head.

CHAPTER 5

TRAINING DAY

I walk through the red door, and I see that Virgil is waiting for me. He hands me a sheath for Cal that I can sling across my back.

"What now?" I ask Virgil.

"We go deeper into Limbo to train before stepping into Hell," he says. He gives me a once over.

Hope he doesn't know about my make-out session with G.

"May I call my mother, please? I need to ask her something," I tell Virgil. He sighs, reaching into his back pants pocket and pulls out my phone.

"Please make it quick," he tells me politely.

I unlock the screen on my phone, going into favorites, pressing "Mom." The phone rings about three times before she picks up.

"Sera?" she asks.

"Mom, what is going on?" I ask quickly.

"Sera, we tried to give you as much of a normal human life as possible, but now you have to face your destiny. Trust in Virgil, he will guide you true. Remember that we love you," and with that, she hangs up.

Fuuuuuuck!

I am beyond hurt and pissed that my parents have lied to me my whole life and didn't bother to once mention the fact that I wasn't even fucking human! Biting down the burning rage that I'm feeling, I compartmentalize the betrayal, sticking it in a box and tabling it for a later date. I can't confront my parents now anyway and I've got much current problems to do deal with.

I give Virgil my phone back. "Lead the way," I tell him, resigned to my current situation. We head downstairs through the dancing crowd. Except for this time, the crowd parts around us, like the parting of the Red Sea. Must be because I got a glowing sword slung on my back or my bright eyes. Either way, my confidence is lifting.

I follow Virgil through another red door and down another dim corridor. We start descending many stairs and several dark hallways until I have no clue how to get back up to the main level.

"This place is huge" I comment. Virgil cracks a grin at me.

"You have not seen anything yet," he responds. *Was he insinuating his dick size?* Nope, not going there, one man's rejection is good enough for one night. Don't want two.

"Why did you kiss me?" Mortified, I feel that my cheeks are on fire. *Why did I blurt that out?*

He stops and turns to me, silver eyes glowing, staring. "You looked so timid and lost. Wanted to give you a confidence boost."

A girl can dream. "I'm not someone to pity so please stop," I say, starting to walk past Virgil. He grabs my arm and brings me against his body.

"I don't pity you," he growls, putting his arms around me, placing his lips on mine. Unlike G's kiss that was animalistic, this kiss is soft but intense.

We both entwine our tongues at the same time, and I again feel that zing! How can I be attracted to two men at the same time? Virgil lifts me up, and I wrap my legs around his waist, straddling him. I somehow lose all inhibitions and propriety after I take my one and only legal drink. He feels good and makes me feel wanted.

I then feel a bulge in his jeans. *Damn! Another big cock.* Must be from drinking the water here. We keep kissing, with me rubbing myself on his cock.

Virgil slowly breaks the kiss and puts me down. He places his forehead on mine. As if he's in pain, he says, "Time is of the essence, and we need to train you to survive Hell." The statement sounds like an apology.

"Okay, let's go" I sigh, giving him a kiss on the cheek and an understanding smile. Virgil turns and starts walking down the corridor with me trailing. Good thing we have further to walk so I can forget the painful throbbing between my legs.

What feels like hours and many more flights down, we finally stop in front of a red door. Virgil twists the knob and pushes open the door, a bright, white light blinds me for a second. "After you," he ushers me in and then follows. Closing the door behind him.

"Ready to get your ass handed to you, little girl?" I hear G's voice from somewhere in the room. The room is white, no furniture, and huge. And it's massive. The room can fit my parents' house twice over lengthwise. I look up and see no ceiling. Just a never-ending corridor that goes up. *Shit!*

I feel G's presence before I catch a glimpse of a blur coming from the right. My body is soaring through the air. Whatever hit me feels like a fucking truck, tossing me into the air like a piece of meat, with me landing on my side. Onto a cement floor. Fucking hard enough to knock the wind out of me. *Oww!*

When I'm finally able to breathe, I stand up slowly to see if I broke any bones. Raising my eyes to Virgil who's still standing near the only door in the room, I ask, "Did you get the license plate number of the truck that hit me?" He gives me a grin filled with pity for my current plight.

I can feel G's presence again, this time behind me. I spin around as fast as I can, but I am still sent flying. This time I'm landing hard on my ass. I sit up and see that G is standing about five feet away from my landing zone smirking at me.

"Save your wise-ass remarks for someone who cares," he tells me.

"You must care since they bother you," I snark.

"Get your ass up, little girl. We're only getting started." I already feel like a big bruise.

"You feel G's presence?" Cal asks in my head. Oh yeah, my magical talking sword.

"Yes."

"Focus on that, his energy," Cal tells me.

"He's doing Mach one and hitting me like a fucking train before I can see him!"

"If you focus hard enough, you will able to see him in the stream," Cal explains.

"Any day now, little girl." Interrupting my internal dialogue with the sword I look over to the owner of the voice. G's body is tense with impatience. Getting up to my feet, I face G. Instead of looking at G with my eyes, I block out all my senses so I can feel his energy.

G's presence is commanding, but his energy signature felt dim, like a dark, rainy day. I then try to feel Virgil's presence. Virgil's energy feels warm and giving, like the sun giving life on a spring day. A different energy signature than G's.

I can feel G's energy starting to move. Refocusing myself and my eyes to him, I can see him running towards me. G is going slow enough for me to move out of the way in the last second. For good measure I stick my foot out to trip G, sending him flying face first into the cement floor twelve feet away. I am feeling some satisfaction when he rolls over and stares at me with shock. *Score one for me!*

He then glares at me and stands up. "Well, well," he says with sarcasm. "Little girl figured out how to see someone in the stream, but can she slip into the stream?" I sigh, feeling deflated. "Get over here, little girl. We are not going to the next phase of your training until you learn how to slip yourself into the stream and hit me."

Shit.

I clear my mind of doubts and let my eyes glaze over; feeling deep inside me, feeling the energy that is my own signature. My power feels like a star, burning extraordinarily bright and extremely hot. Now to propel it.

I focus on G's energy, using it like a magnet. I open my eyes, and I let go. It feels like half a minute to me, running towards G's energy location and slamming balls to the wall into it. I hear a grunt, and I refocus my eyes to see G flying twenty feet away from me. Landing on his ass. Hard. *Yes!*

There's clapping behind me. I turn to see Virgil clapping and smiling. I give him a full smile in return before returning my attention back to G. He's already on his feet, glaring at me with his glowing green eyes. "Again," he orders.

I don't let myself get cocky. I focus inside myself again, feeling G's energy, except this time he's on the move, in the stream. Then I get an idea.

I let myself go, but instead of using G as a magnet, I allow myself to feel like a pinball. Using the walls to bounce me around to change directions and trying to anticipate G's course. I see G, and I somehow know where he's about to change direction again. I have to beat him to the spot.

Somewhere, deep within me, I ask for more power. Feeling a surge of light and heat, my speed explodes to a whole new level. I go from hyper-speed to ludicrous speed. Spaceballs anyone?

I hit the spot that I knew G was about to turn at, and it was like a train hitting a VW Bug. The Bug would go splat. I hit G so hard that I send him sailing across the length of two football fields, hitting the far wall with a splat! *Oops!*

I slip out of the stream and stop to see Virgil's reaction. He's staring at me, his mouth hanging open, eyes wide with shock. "Will he be okay?" I ask Virgil.

"Uh!?" is all that Virgil responds with.

I look to the far wall, and I see G walking towards me. Slowly. When he finally gets to me, he's looking at me like I am a freak. "How the fuck did you do that?" he asks.

"I don't know," I say with a shrug. "I was able to anticipate your location and asked for more energy. I somehow got the burst of speed I needed to get to the location before you," I respond. G shakes his head, with a bewildering look on his face.

Virgil chimes in, "It's time she took a break, Gabriel." G nods his head in agreement. Virgil starts walking towards me, but G gives him a sharp look, making him stop.

"She'll come with me," G commands. All Virgil could do was press his lips together and then turns to walk out the door.

G walks towards the same door with me in tow. Out of the training room, G turns left and walks. I follow G down the corridor, and G stops in front of another red door.

He opens the door and steps through with me behind. The second I pass the thresh-hold, the door automatically shuts and locks behind me. I'm locked in a room with G. *Oh no!*

Looking around the room, I see a big bed, covered in white sheets, and an open doorway going into a bathroom. No door. There is also a small kitchenette with a full-size fridge on the other side of the room. My stomach starts to rumble. I unsling Cal, placing the sword next to the door before walking to the refrigerator, opening it.

The refrigerator is stocked with pre-made sandwiches, salads, and bottles of water. I grab a water bottle and a sandwich and plop down at the small table. I'm starving, so I dig in. The sandwich is delicious.

"Get some sleep," G orders, "you will have a longer and harder session in a few hours."

Taking a deep breath, I ask, "Where are you sleeping?" G gives me a wicked grin and lays down, still clothed, on the only bed in the room.

G lifts his head up, looking at me like I am an idiot. "I'm not going to touch you. Little boys are not my thing, remember?" he says with disgust. I'm too fucking tired to care about his snide comments. I walk to the other side of the bed, sitting down to take my boots off. Pulling the top sheet back, I crawl underneath the pristine white sheets. I'm out when my head hits the pillow.

I open my eyes, coming to awareness of the room I'm in. I am pressing against something warm and hard. There is an arm draped over my waist. *G's spooning me?* I start wiggling away from G, but his arm tightens, pulling me closer to his body.

I wiggle a little harder, hoping that he wakes up and doesn't crush me with his tree stump arms in the process. "Stop wiggling your ass against my dick, little girl, or you are going to regret what comes next," G growls in my ear.

I sigh, exasperated that I'm in this fucking predicament. *Why me?*

"I'm not the one holding and spooning you. Please let me go?" I ask quietly.

"All in good time" is G's response.

"You told me that you were not attracted to me. Why keep holding me then?" I keep pushing, reminding him of his disgust towards me.

Instead of letting me go, he brings me closer to him. I turn my head towards his, wondering if he's even awake. G's glowing green eyes are open and staring into mine.

Definitely awake.

With his strength like it weighs nothing, G easily flips my body towards him and starts kissing my neck. G is a master seducer, because I start melting into his arms. When he feels the rigidness in my body relaxing, he moves from my neck to my lips, kissing me deeply. I kiss him back, taking in his scent that reminds me of open country air, crisp and clean.

Our kiss is slow and exploratory like we have all the time in the world. But we don't because there's a knock on the door. "Gabriel?" Virgil's voice is muffled by the door. "Are you and Sera ready?" G stops kissing and looks down at me. I look back at him and give him a small grin.

He frowns, then roughly pushes me away from him. G springs out of bed, his boots still on, giving me a disgusted look, probably remembering his self-proclamation that he is not attracted to me what-so-ever, while walking to the door and yanking it open. G marches past a surprised Virgil.

What did I do now?

Virgil looks at me questioningly. I shrug my shoulders and shake my head like I have no clue what crawled up G's ass. I move to my side of the bed. Grabbing my boots, I put them on and then walk over to Cal to sling the sword across my back. I head out the open doorway, shutting the door behind me.

The walk to the training room is in silence. I'm still trying to wrap my head around G's bipolar mood swings. When we reach the door to the training room, I turn to Virgil and ask, "What is the stream by the way? I was too tired to ask yesterday."

Opening the door and letting me walk through first, Virgil replies, "The stream is like a corridor through normal space and time. Time moves much slower. So, moving fast in the stream causes you to move inhumanly fast in normal space in time."

Next question: "How did I move faster than G yesterday?"

Virgil grins at me and says, "You're very powerful. You must have been able to slow the corridor even more, which takes a lot of energy, to be able to go that much faster."

I nod my head in understanding Virgil's simplified explanation. Virgil can definitely replace Neil Tyson Degrassi in those science documentaries.

"Thank you for answering my questions," I say to Virgil with a smile.

"Anytime," he answers back with another grin. He's so handsome and charming!

Speaking of handsome, I start feeling out for G's energy, realizing he's heading towards me in the stream. Giving Virgil a quick peck on the cheek, I slip into the stream.

For hours we are in the stream, with G trying to catch me to knock me on my ass. *G definitely needs to get a new hobby.*

I can feel my energy getting low, and I know that I will need to stop soon. "Stop!" I hear G command. I stay, time going back to normal, my body fatigued.

"We will now spar with our swords," he states. I'm already tired! "If you're able to draw my blood, your training is done."

Sadistic prick!

G pulls a fucking huge-ass, black broadsword from behind him. Of course. "No wonder you're such a tyrannical asshole. If I had wings plus a broadsword stuck up my ass, I would be a total prick also," I say with a smile. I hear Virgil coughing and trying to hold in his laughter. G looks like he's about to skewer me with that massive black broadsword. *Fuck.*

I focus on G's energy, feeling him move in the stream. I instinctively roll out of the way. "Let me out to play," Cal sings. I grab the hilt and pull Cal out, using two hands to hold the sword in front of me. I get into a fighting stance that I have seen in movies.

I notice that the blade is glowing a greenish color. No time to think about that while getting to my feet. "Bring it on, bitch," I growl at G. He cracks a small grin before going back into the stream.

I focus on his energy, and I let instinct take over to dodge his assault. He then starts attacking me with his sword, and Cal is controlling me, blocking his blows. I hear a hum coming from Cal, and I start humming along also. I am at peace, even though I know that G is out for blood. Probably because he's still angry that he broke his own vows about touching me in bed this morning.

I am so peaceful in fact that when I jump to avoid G's leg from trying swipe my legs out from under me, I don't come down. I am hovering. *Why am I flying?!*

I turn my head and see a wing made of pure fire. Turning my head the other way and I see the same fucking thing. I panic, and the wings disappear. I drop three feet to the floor. "What the fuck was that?!" I yell.

My fiery wings and outburst didn't stop G from attacking me, though. I let instinct and Cal take over again until I expect G's stroke with his enormous broadsword. Going ludicrous speed again, I move to the side and swipe Cal across G's hand. Giving him a small cut that swelled up with a little blood. *Score two for me!*

We both stop and he looks at me incredulously. I have a feeling no one has ever bested him in a sword fight before.

G turns to Virgil. "She's rapidly evolving," Virgil says to G.

"Can't believe The Creator entrusted this little girl with this mission," G mutters.

I am approaching G, feeling rage burning in my gut. I'm tired of G's condescension towards me. "My name is not 'little girl,' you fucking twat!" I spit out. "It's Seraphim, Sera to my friends. That's not you, asshole." I put Cal back in the sheath.

"Are we done here?" I ask. "I definitely need to eat, drink, shower, and sleep before starting this journey." I'm now exhausted. The amount of time training, shock, and the energy of fighting with G have completely drained me.

G turns to Virgil and says, "Get everything ready. We leave in a few hours." He then turns to me and commands, "You, come with me." And walks to the red door. He opens it and I follow, giving Virgil a smile before leaving. He smiles back, making my stomach flutter. *Why can't I stay with him instead?*

I follow G down the corridor back to the room we shared the night before. Once we get the room, G opens the door, and I notice that that the cut on his hand is gone. G steps through the doorway with me in tow. Taking Cal off, I place it in the same spot as the night before.

I look around noticing that someone made up the bed. I walk over to the fridge, open it, grab another water and a different sandwich, and sit down at the small table. I devour the sandwich. I'm still hungry, so I get up and grab a different sandwich. I take my time eating this one.

I didn't realize G has taken a shower until he is standing at the open doorway, with only a towel around his waist. He is a fantasy come true with eight-pack abs and a broad chest and skin that has been bronzed by the sun. I shake my head, trying to clear the vision that's making me wet below. I go back to eating, ignoring G.

"You will be getting new clothes in a few hours. I'm going to bed," I hear G say. I keep silent while I listen to sheets being pulled back then adjusting. When I hear heavy breathing, I get up and go into the bathroom.

I take a quick, hot shower. Easing some of the aches in my arms and legs from my long ass training session with G. Since I have no clean clothes, I wrap myself in a towel. Leaving the bathroom, I walk to the other side of the bed. I pull the sheets back, lie down, and take the damp cloth off, placing it on the floor. I then roll to the side and drift off to sleep.

I dream of being in a beautiful field with a bright blue sky and the sun beating down on my skin. I am feeling warm and happy. I then notice that someone is touching me, pleasing me with their hands. Rubbing the pleasure spot on my pussy and a mouth gently sucking my neck, making me moan and wet. I want more.

And then I open my eyes, realizing it's not a dream. There is a warm, naked body behind me with a massive erect cock rubbing into my back. Fingers are rubbing my clit, making me so wet and needy that I don't care that it's G. All I can feel is the pleasure. And now I know I definitely want more.

I open my legs wider to give his fingers better access to my entrance. Wanting to be filled by them. He complies by sticking in one finger, then two, rubbing the walls of my pussy and spot at the same time.

I can feel a pressure building and growing, like a dam about to burst. I suddenly convulse while screaming out at the same time. Wave after wave of pleasure hits me while the muscles in my pussy are squeezing his fingers. My first orgasm. And I definitely want another one.

Before I know what I am doing, I turn my body with G's fingers still inside me and I kiss him. I then get bold by trying to wrap my fingers around his huge cock. He's incredibly big, but it doesn't stop me from massaging his length.

He starts kissing me back with such need and intensity that all I could do is hold on to his cock. He scoots his massive body over mine, settling between my legs. His huge cock nudging at my entrance. And with one thrust, tears into me.

I break the kiss, crying out, tears spilling from the sides of my eyes because all I can feel is the pain. He looks down at me, as if actually seeing me for the first time. With understanding dawning on his face, he says, "You really are a virgin." Not a question but a statement. "Fuck," he says quietly while trying to withdraw from me.

I wrap my legs around his waist, stopping him. The pain is starting to lessen. "Uh uh," I admonish him. "Finish what you fucking started." I look at him, waiting.

"Tell me when the pain is bearable," he states, tenderly wiping the tears from my eyes. The only time he's ever been kind and gentle with me. It takes another minute to adjust to his size, but I give him the nod when I'm ready.

He slowly starts rocking cock into me. I feel incredibly full, but the pain is beginning to turn to pleasure and I'm meeting his thrusts. G then switches gears and thrusts harder and faster into me.

That sweet building of pressure I felt before with his fingers is starting again. "Oh God, I'm going to come!" I tell him. He drives harder and faster.

"That's my good little girl, squeeze my dick," he tells me.

I comply, roaring with pleasure and release, feeling like my soul flew to heaven and back. My pussy is squeezing his big cock, feeling like it can't get enough.

And then he really starts pounding into me. Another orgasm rips through me before I can recover from the first one. "You're so beautiful and tight," he tells me. "You're going to make me come hard like the good little girl you are," he growls and here comes orgasm number three. This time I hear him moaning, finding his own release, shooting his cum deep within me.

He slows his thrusting until he stops. He does not look at me as he pulls out with a wet pop, leaving me empty but sated. He moves to his side of the bed, turning onto his side with his back facing me. I went from feeling wanted to feeling like a used condom. *God that hurts!*

From the pain by G's callousness of what we did, I am feeling like I am being kicked in the chest. A few tears spill out. *Why is he always extremely hot or cold to me?* Then it dawns on me. He was using me. How could I be so fucking stupid! I refuse to cry in front of G.

Getting out of the bed, I walk naked to the bathroom with the evidence of our fucking dripping down my legs onto the floor. I don't give a shit at this point.

This time I take a very long shower, washing all evidence of my stupidity away. Quietly crying to get rid of the pain in my chest while hardening my heart and soul in the process. *Hope G can't hear the unwarranted pain he has caused me.*

Would have lost my virginity sooner if I found a guy who is actually attracted to me and I to him. I thought G felt some kind of attraction towards me when he told me that I was beautiful. *Geez! I'm so naive!*

I'm going to have to block him out and only speak to him only when need be. I'm done with his mind games! Never having sex with him again.

I hear a knock at the open doorway. "New clothes are here. Leaving them on the counter," G calls to me, sounding indifferent.

"Thank you!" I say as if nothing has happened. *I can pretend also.*

I hear him walk out. I turn off the shower water and step out. All the articles of clothing on the counter are new except my boots. Everything is military-style and in black. Fits my mood.

The new nylon T-shirt and tactical cargo pants fit perfectly. I even got a sports bra to keep me strapped in. Well, at least I will fight comfortably.

I walk out of the bathroom, seeing that G is ready, standing near the door waiting for me. I get Cal and strap it to my back. "We going?" I ask G.

I then notice G looking at the bed. There is a nice, wet red stain on the pristine white sheets, a visual reminder to me of what recently happened. I roll my eyes. It's in the past. Another thing to compartmentalize and table. "Well?" I ask again. G clenches his jaw and turns, opening the door.

Virgil is standing right in front of the door, waiting for us. He looks gorgeous in his dark military style getup. I walk past G keeping my head up, showing that he cannot hurt me, and past Virgil. I walk a few steps, noticing that both men are not following or taking the lead.

I turn around. I see Virgil's face and he looks pissed, and G is looking straight back at him with no expression. What can I say? I'm always up for stirring the pot. Rolling my eyes, I walk back over to the two men, looking like they're about throw fists at each other.

"Let's get this over with, shall we?" I say politely. I first address Virgil "Yes, G fucked me, making me no longer a virgin. But he's made it perfectly clear that he wants nothing to do with me and I'm absolutely fine with that. Now, Virgil, if you still want me, I would be more than happy to be with you. You have been extremely nice and gentle to me. Sometimes," I add. "But it's been better than how that fucker has treated me," I say, pointing at G.

Now its G's turn. "G, I appreciate that you thought me a slut and that I automatically knew how to use my powers to seduce you. Now that I know you lack in all things, especially intelligence, I forgive you, but will not fuck you again. Ever." Emphasizing on the "ever." I could see anger and frustration on G's face as he's clenching his jaw. Don't know why he would feel that way?

"Well," I continue, "now we that we got that issue out of the way, can we please continue to the gate and get this shit over with? After you" I motion to both men. The fun is just getting started.

CHAPTER 6

LAST STOP BEFORE HELL

All three of us walk in uncomfortable silence. All I can hear is my boots hitting the cement floor, echoing around me. I can't stop thinking about the soreness between my legs; trying to ignore the discomfort. *I hope the soreness and pain in my chest leave very soon.*

I'm starting to feel a strange energy in the air. Almost like knowing when a thunderstorm is about to hit. "What is that? I can feel energy like it's almost tangible," I say to no one in particular.

"It's the door," Virgil replies. "It's made of pure energy, the energy that you can now tune in to and use once you get strong enough to control it.". Walking down the dim corridor did nothing but help increase my anxiety.

'Relax little one,' Cal says smoothly into my head. 'All will be well. Breath.' I start taking deep breaths. Good thing I've done some yoga and Pilates to help control my breathing and ease my anxiety. 'Much better," Cal soothes. *A sword to calm me down definitely fits this strange situation.*

We finally reach a considerable set of, wait for it, red double doors. Red, the color of fresh blood, almost like the stain on G's white sheets. *Blocking that out! Concentrate on the task in front of you! Like both men' hot asses! Ugh! What is wrong with me?*

It's like the hormones and sexual drive I never had in my teen years decided to bombard me now, all at once! I need to get this job done as fast as possible so I can get away from these men. Before I get hurt. Bad.

On the floor next to the doors are three, huge hiking backpacks. Each complete with a rolled up sleeping bag, and filled to the brim with what I'm guessing are essential supplies.

Glad that riding a bike a couple of miles a day prepared me for a long fucking hike. Into Hell. And those packs look heavy.

Virgil picks up a pack like it weighs nothing. "Sera, please step forward and turn around," Virgil says to me. I give him a small grin.

"If you wanted to stare at my ass you don't need to ask," teasing him. Virgil smiles at me, making my stomach somersault. I hear a snort beside me, but I don't bother looking at G.

I turn around, and Virgil places the pack on my back. I thread my arms through the shoulder straps until both the straps settle onto my shoulders.

The bag weighs nothing because I can't feel any weight on my shoulders or back. I give Virgil a confused look while he's adjusting the straps in front of me. "Why is the pack so light?" I ask him.

Before he can answer G says, "You were given the Holy Fire shot and the power of Excalibur. You are faster, stronger, and powerful. One of the most powerful beings in existence. A mere 150 pounds should feel like air to you." I look over at G, and he looks grim. *Whatever.*

I turn back and stare into Virgil's silver swirling eyes. Reminds me of molten silver. Feeling bold, I kiss him on the mouth, a sweet innocent kiss. Virgil groans, and pulls me in, possessing my mouth.

I even forgot G was there until I heard him say, "You gonna fuck her here or do want to wait a little later when we take a break?" I stop kissing Virgil, looking over at G with a huge smile.

"What a wonderful idea G! Glad we got a fucking plan before stepping into Hell." I love it when I can get a pun in. "And when I say 'fucking' it definitely does not include you!"

I see a dark shadow cross G's face and his glowing green eyes flaring. It looks like he's struggling to control his wrath aimed at me. I turn back to Virgil. "Ready?" I ask him. He has no fear of G's wrath because he gives me a soft peck on the lips.

"Ready," he replies. I turn towards the door waiting for one of the guys to open it.

"Only you can open the door," Virgil says.

"Oh! Okay?" unsure of why that is, I touch the handle and words appear in big golden script. 'Abandon all hope, those who enter here.' *Nice.* I twist the handle and push the massive door open. I see nothing but darkness. There is no turning back now. I step through. God help us.

The Love Boat

After walking in a few steps, the darkness turns into a dark grey, misty, miserable place. A place that has never seen sunlight. I can see nothing because of the thickness of the fog. The air smells stale and moldy.

I then feel the presence of Virgil and G on either side of me and hear the enormous door slam shut. It felt like the air got sucked out of this cold, rank, place. "Where to?" I whisper.

"Straight," says Virgil. I start walking, not hearing a sound except for our boots hitting the ground.

It seems like hours have passed, seeing nothing but dense fog. I start hearing the soft lapping of water. "You hear that?" I ask.

"The River Styx," both men say in unison. I've mentioned that I read, a lot, and I've read Homer's the Odyssey.

"The same River Styx with the ferryman named Charon, taking souls who can pay the fee, across to Hades?" I ask.

"Well, at least you're well read and know mythology," G comments. *Blow me!* As we get closer to the sound of water, the fog starts lifting.

The stench yet becomes is horrible, like the smell of something died and decided to keep rotting in Hell.

We keep walking forward until I see a small lamp hanging from a post. Getting closer turns out the lamp is on a post attached to a small, haphazard dock. A couple of boards either rotted away because of the awful smell or the thick fog got hungry. Don't want to know either way.

Carefully, we walk onto the dock, testing the boards still present to see if they can hold our weight. I then see an old bell where you have to swing the chord to ring it. "What, no 'For service, please ring the bell,' sign?" I quip. I turn to look at Virgil and see him shaking his head and smiling. I then look at G. Nothing. At least one of them gets me.

Okay, I ring the bell, and that fucker is loud. Sounds like I pulled 'Big Marie's' chord like I was the Hunchback of Notre Dame. The sound keeps echoing across the black River Styx. And we wait.

We don't wait long because out of the dark dead sea comes our ride. The ship looks like an Ancient Greek bireme, with two levels of oars sticking out and rowing in sync to a rhythm we cannot hear. As the boat turns and aligns to the dock with smooth precision, I catch a glimpse of the infamous ferryman Charon.

I was expecting the grim reaper who was always depicted as a male skeleton in black robes. Instead, I see a pale, beautiful woman with unnaturally white hair, straight as a board going all the way down her back, and eyes as black as the River Styx.

She is wearing soft black leather pants and a leather halter top that looks like it is painted on her; showing off her voluptuous cleavage. She could easily fill a double D size bra. Not that I'm complaining, since I can fill a D cup myself; but I refuse to look at either of the two men beside me, knowing they probably have hard-ons for her.

The gangplank lowers and down the wet dream descends. Charon's eyes start to glow when she gazes at us three and then stops; her gaze pointedly stays on me. "You are not dead and thus cannot board." Of course, she sounds like a rock star and of course I wasn't surprised to what she says to the men, "You two can board my boat anytime." *Gross.*

"Let's go," G states to Charon, his voice filled with lust. *Seriously?*

Virgil, on the other hand, says "She has free passage, as we are all on official Heaven business. You do know who I am and what my job is right?" I look at Virgil and back to Debbie does Dallas. Her face is grim and says through clenched teeth "Fine, welcome aboard." *Bitch.*

Of course, I couldn't let her attitude go unchecked. "Will there be 24-hour room service and a buffet on this lovely cruise?" I quip.

She gives me a look of pure loathing, but then turns her attention on G and gives him a flirtatious smile, "Follow me please." I can only roll my eyes and grind my teeth. *Don't want to be kicked off the cruise before boarding.*

G, of course, follows her up the gangplank like a fucking dog. *Typical.* Both Virgil and I follow. When we get onto the deck, I notice a wooden building like structure with doors and numbers stenciled into each entry. I also realize that the stench of the River Styx doesn't follow us onto the ship.

Charon takes G by the hand and leads him to door number one. She turns to look at Virgil and me. "You are in rooms two and three. Don't get lost and don't knock on this door at all. We have seven days to reach the First Circle. Have a wonderful trip!" she says sarcastically. And with that, she opens the door and walks in with G in tow. Door slamming shut behind them. *Cunt!*

I have a hard time keeping my jealousy under control, but feeling Virgil's presence behind me helps calms me down. I put on a happy face and turn to him. "Your room or mine?" I ask.

We end up in room number three. Didn't want to hear G getting it on with a whore from Hell. Just saying.

The room is actually very luxurious and spacious. Like a suite at Cesar's hotel in Vegas kind of roomy. "How the fuck does this room even fit on this boat?" I turn and ask Virgil.

"We are in a place where time and space are infinite. With enough power and control you can create any space you want," he explains. Okay, sounds reasonable to me.

Space is adorned in grey marble with naked statues of gods and goddesses in the corners. There are picture windows with a view of a vast sunlit ocean painted on the walls. And the paintings look so realistic that the water is actually rising and falling in time with the rocking of the ship. *Not going dwell on it.*

We dump our belongings on the floor, including Cal. Not worried that someone would try to steal a holy sword on a boat heading to Hell.

I take Virgil's hand and lead him to a set of double doors which I can only assume is the master bedroom. I open the door and see a massive bed and a large open doorway that could only lead to the bathroom. What is it with the lack of privacy?

I turn to Virgil and all the jealousy I felt for G flew out of my mind when I saw the raw lust on Virgil's face. Wow, I'm getting sopping wet. He takes both my hands, pulls me towards him so I can wrap my arms around his body and I stare up at him. He makes me feel like I'm the only girl in the universe he wants.

He slowly brings his head down to mine, but I take the initiative and meet him halfway. Our lips crash into each other. Tongues are starting to dance. So different from G. Tender yet passionate. He hugs my body closer to his, molding me against him. I groan because it feels so good to be wanted.

I guess my groan turned him on even more because he starts backing us up until the bed hits me in the back of the knees and I fall back with him on top of me. Our kissing becomes intense. I put my hands under his shirt, wanting to feel his muscles ripple under the touch of my hands. It was his turn to groan.

I start tugging his shirt up, wanting it off so I can see his beautiful body. He breaks our kiss to pull his shirt over his head. Wow, he's gorgeous with a defined chest and an impressive six-pack with golden skin. I start to trace my fingers around each ab muscle, observing how they quiver and then I started kissing them. I've never felt so empowered.

I then feel a tugging of my shirt which I am more than happy to remove, wanting to feel his skin on mine. Of course, the sports bra becomes a challenge, but like the shirt, I pull it over my head, my breasts bouncing freely. I forgot how restrained my boobs get in those things.

Virgil stares at my chest and then lowers his head down to put my nipple in his mouth. Like a line of fire going down to the junction between my legs.

While he's paying attention to my nipples, I reach in between us to put my hand into his pants. His girth is making me question about putting him inside me. And he likes going commando. I start undoing his web belt and buttons. He stops suddenly and turns to take off his boots and removes his pants.

He then removes my boots, and I unbuckle my own web belt and undue the pant buttons. Virgil tugs the pants off me, leaving me in my underwear. He then climbs over on top of me, tracing a finger from my nipple, down my stomach, to the aching part between my legs.

Virgil dips his hand into my underwear until he feels my slick folds and the tiny nub begging for his attention. "So beautiful and wet for me," he murmurs.

Virgil then kisses me and starts trailing kisses down my body. Stopping at each breast to give them attention and then keeps kissing down my stomach until he hits my panty line. "These need to go," he states and pulls them off me. I am now fully exposed for his perusal. "So fucking beautiful," he says.

He returns to the location of where he left off kissing me. He takes my leg and lifts it over his head, so he's in between my legs. I see he's looking hungrily at my wet pussy. Makes me want to come right now.

He starts kissing the inside of my leg and then I feel his warm breath on my folds. His tongue starts swirling around on my clit, making me moan with pleasure. I must have died for this to be happening to me!

He keeps on teasing me with his tongue and then drags my body closer to suck on my clit. I feel that exquisite pressure is starting to build and then he sticks his two fingers in me, fucking me, while his mouth is performing magic on my clit. The dam breaks and I scream with pleasure, the muscles in my pussy squeezing and I know I need more.

Virgil looks up at me, his silver eyes swirling, a mischievous grin on his face. I can only grin back as he crawls up to me, nestling his hips between my legs, his cock at my throbbing entrance, waiting for him to enter me.

He kisses me slowly, and I taste myself on his lips. I find it really hot. I then feel the head of his cock nudging into me. He's so big! He takes his time pushing into me, kissing me and encouraging me to take more of him until he's all the way to the hilt. He's so big and wide, I feel him stretching me to the fullest.

Then I start moving, setting a rhythm that turns the fullness to extreme pleasure. When Virgil hears me moaning, he takes over, thrusting into me, creating the pressure that's going to throw me into sweet rapture.

"Oh, Virgil!" I yell, "I'm going to come so hard! Don't stop!"

"Never," he replies. "Come for me baby," he says. I shatter, and I felt like my soul left my body. My pussy is squeezing his cock, wanting more. "You want more?" Virgil asks me. *Did he just hear my thoughts?*

I can only nod my head, yes, and then he starts to twirl his hips around and reaches in between us to use his thumb to rub on my clit. "Oh Fuck!" I shout as another orgasm rips down my body. I don't know how many more orgasms my body can take, but it seems that Virgil wants to find out.

"More?" he asks.

"Yes please," I beg. I also want to see how many orgasms he can get out of me.

He pulls out, grabs my waist and flips me onto my stomach, lifting my ass into the air, spreading my knees wide, fully exposing my dripping wet pussy. I then feel him pushing into me from behind. He drives into me deeper, feeling so fucking good.

He starts pounding my pussy. I orgasmed two more times. By the last one, my body was weak, and my pussy is getting sore. I think Virgil senses my exhaustion because he then really starts to pound into me, his balls slapping against my ass. The pressure that was building causes an orgasm so big that I see stars and heard his cry as well as feeling his hot semen squirting into me.

I collapse into a heap of pure exhaustion. Virgil rolls to the side, bringing the comforter around us, tucking me close to him and kisses me on the cheek. *A girl can get used to this!*

I drift off to sleep.

CHAPTER 7

More Fucking Training

I come to with a sound of something or someone pounding on a door. I crack my eyes open and feel Virgil's arms tighten around me. I would love to drift back to sleep, but the pounding on the door doesn't stop. I get up, putting my clothes on and trudge to the door barefoot. Someone has better died because I'm tired and deliciously sore in all the right places.

I open the door and G is standing there, black hair perfectly trimmed and groomed, face cleanly shaved. He's looking refreshed and ready for a new day. "Yes G?" I ask bitchily.

"Where's Virgil?" he asks.

"In the bed where I left him. Why?" The tone in my voice is reflecting how tired I am after last night's activities with Virgil.

The dark look that I saw on G's face before walking through the door into Hell crosses his features. "What do you want G?" The hot and cold signals from G are definitely starting to irritate me. I'd rather be anywhere but here talking to him right now.

"Finish getting dressed. Training time," he commands.

"Awesome!" I say sarcastically.

I close the door and head to the bathroom. I need a few minutes to get my mind into the game. After some quick grooming, I put my boots on and kiss my sleeping Virgil. *Whoa? My sleeping Virgil? Nope, not going there!* I need to keep myself emotionally detached. This could all be a fling for him like it was for G.

I strap Cal on and walk out the door. Another shitty day on the River Styx. No sunlight, only fog, and shadows. G is standing near the door entrance. He is wearing black tactical cargo pants and boots, the pants hugging his hips, held up by a web belt. The black nylon t-shirt is clutching his massive chest, accenting his bulging arms. *If he weren't such an asshole, he would be perfect!*

Upon seeing me, he turns on his heel to the right and starts walking. I sigh and follow him. Feeling depressed, I slump my shoulders until I recall how Virgil held me when we slept. The thought helps put some spring into my step.

G stops in front of a set of double doors, pull them open and walk in. I follow him into what looks like a large boxing gym, complete with life-size dummies and padding all over the walls and floor.

"Take the sword off," G commands gruffly. I remove Cal and place it near the door. I turn back to face G, only to be flung like a rag doll into a side wall. *Uh, ouch?!*

Now I know what the padding is for. Getting up and looking at G, I notice that he hasn't moved at all. "What the fuck dude?!" I demand.

He shrugs and says, "I have an affinity for air. I lifted and tossed you like a feather. I will teach you to tap into your energy that will help us fight the creatures that we are going to run into while descending into the nine circles of Hell." *Tap into my energy? This should be easy.* Famous last words.

For what feels like hours, G has me doing all types of physical activities until I'm covered in sweat, and my muscles are fatigued. He created a big circle of stations around the open gym floor. One station for sit-ups, the next station for push-ups, etc., and I had to run once around the whole perimeter of the stations to get to the next station.

After one complete circuit, G would add 5 more sets for each station that I had to complete. After the fourth circuit, I started going into muscle fatigue. The fact that I'm completely out of shape for this type of physical activity annoys the shit out of me!

"What the fuck does running my ass into the ground have anything to do with using energy?" I ask G, sounding annoyed.

"The stronger your body, the longer you can use your energy. Everything has a price. The energy you use to perform the impossible needs a lot of physical energy and could suck you dry. You need to have the endurance to keep on fighting until you are safe to re-energize." G explains. *Okay.*

He places a feather in the center of a large sparring mat. "Now," G says to me, "tap into your energy and move the feather." *No fucking way!*

I stare at the feather, trying anything to make it move. I can't feel anything, no energy, nothing. Feeling too much has gone by, I concentrate harder. There is sweat is beading down my face, between my breasts, and down the front and back of my whole body while I'm straining to do what G wants.

I hear G sigh and say "Wow, you really are a pathetic little girl. Can't even move a feather." I try to ignore his comment, focusing on the feather. But he keeps going. "No wonder you're a one time fuck. I had a real woman last night, and I feel sorry that Virgil got stuck fucking a little girl that looks more like a boy." *THAT IS IT!*

Reaching deep down inside me, fucking pissed that he thinks he can talk to me like that is when I felt it. Energy, a well of energy begging to be tapped. And tap it I will.

In the blink of an eye, I spin towards G, and I feel the air like it was play-dough, ready to be molded into anything I wanted. I mold it into a giant fucking ball, big enough to slam G into the wall. He hits the wall hard enough to shake the room. But I don't let go, I keep him held against the wall, five feet up. *He's fucked with the wrong bitch!*

"Listen dickless," I snarl. "I have had enough of your shit! Don't ever talk to me like that again! Not my fault that you wanted nothing to do with me after you fucked me, but I won't let that situation, or you break me. I am done for the day." I take the air mold holding G and use it to launch him back to the sparring mat.

I make sure he lands on his ass, right next to the feather so the impact can cause the feather to lift up and float down. "Look! I moved the feather!" I say with bitchiness, walking to the door and retrieving Cal. Pulling the door open and swaggering out, "Have a good rest of the day with Charon!" I call over my shoulder sweetly and letting the door slam shut behind me. Time to eat, shower, and sleep.

CHAPTER 8

NOTHING BUT THE TRUTH

When I get back to room three, I see Virgil sitting on a couch, reading an old manuscript. He glances up at me, noticing how sweaty I am. "Training with G," I tell him. "I kicked his ass. Again." Virgil cracks a huge smile at me, making my chest flutter. He's so beautiful! "I need to take a shower and eat lots of food," I tell him. I then hear a knock on the door. I roll my eyes, wondering what G wants now.

I turn and open the door expecting G. Instead it was Charon. "Yes?" I ask her.

"May I come in?" she politely asks. Dumbstruck at her sudden politeness, I step aside and notice she's wearing a different leather outfit as she walks in, but the outfit still looks like it was painted on her. *G must have had a bitch of a time getting her naked. Nope, not going there!*

Closing the door and turning to Charon, I fold my arms over my chest, waiting patiently for her to start talking. She spins around, facing me. "Listen," she says, "I figured out who you truly were last night when

G refused to touch me, telling me he had no interest." *Why the fuck did he tell me he slept with her?*

Charon turns to Virgil, "Does she know?" asking him.

"Know what?" I demand, the shock of G's lie immediately dissipating.

Charon turns back to me, black eyes studying me, seeing the question on my face. "The eight souls you save will be your mates, wanting no other but you. They will remain eternally yours after having you, helping you reach your full power." *Mates!*

I turn to Virgil. "Is this true?" I angrily demand. He looks at me, his expression serious " Yes," he replies.

"I'm taking a shower!" I say, stomping off to the bathroom, too exhausted to deal with this shit.

The bathroom is luxurious. Decorated in pink marble walls, a pebbled floor, and complete with a walk-in rain shower and a huge tub with jets.

I notice a variety of soaps and oils lining the tub. I turn the tub water on, letting it get warm before I stop the drain and start pouring the oils in, each creating different color bubbles. I undress, my clothes reeking and damp with sweat, and step into the warm water; the bubbles are tickling my legs. I sit down, letting the water raise high enough so I can turn on the jets to massage my aching body. I definitely needed this!

I let the water rise to my neck before turning it off, and I sit there in bliss allowing my head clear of the shit that I was told. *Why did G have sex with me if he knew about the mates thing?*

That's when I decide to confront him after I am done bathing and had a bite to eat. After my hands and feet are prunes, I get out, opening the drain to empty the tub. I am feeling much, much better!

Not feel like rummaging through my backpack for new clothes, I opt to put on the blood red silk robe that is hanging in the linen closet. I overlap the sides of the robe, keeping it closed with a bow knot. The bottom of the robe ends above my knees. I decide to go commando as well.

I walk out of the bathroom and bedroom with a purpose in my stride. And then I stop short to see that a buffet table, a sizeable fucking buffet table, is already set up with everything that I love to eat set out from appetizers to desserts.

I pick up a plate and start loading it. I'm beyond hungry. It was then I realized that the room was empty. No Virgil and Charon present. Not caring about anything but my need for sustenance, I dig in.

I eat until I get that bloated feeling. The food is beyond delicious. I wipe my hands and face, plop my napkin on the plate, stand up and walk out the door. Heading to room one. *Time to settle this.*

When I get to G's room, I knock, waiting for the door to open. I wait for a minute or two and tap again. This time louder and more insistent, hitting until I see the handle turn. The door opens and in front of me is a half-naked G. His well well-defined chest and an eight-pack, covered in lightly bronze skin.

I swallow hard because I know I'm in trouble, my attraction for him has not diminished. "What do you want?" not bothering to hide his annoyance.

Flipping my hands up, "Peace," I say. "May I come in?"

He turns, walking into the room and I follow him in, closing the door. His place is much different from room three. Just as significant but more like a New York suite, with modern decor and a lot of straight lines.

G turns around and looks me up and down. Something flared in those glowing green eyes. I cross my arms and ask him point blank, "Did you know that you would become my mate if we had sex?"

"Yes," he replies.

"Then why have you been treating me like shit, trying to make me hate you?" I demand.

"Because I didn't want it to be true. I wanted to be free to do whoever and whatever I want." He says truthfully.

"You still can," I tell him, "I'm not going to force you to stay with me, making you miserable. If you want to go, go." I tell him.

"I fucking can't!" he yells, the anger and frustration clearly showing on his face. "Before we had sex I thought you were an itch that just needed to be scratched. After we had sex, you are the only thing on my mind! I can't be physically far from you without feeling sick and having a goddamn panic attack! When I tried being with Charon, I wished it was you! I couldn't even pretend it was you because she doesn't even smell like you! It's like you imprinted on my soul!" *What can I say to that?*

The silence in the room is deafening. My heart is pounding in my head, not knowing what to do. "G, I'm sorry," I finally say, feeling deflated, a pain in my chest, my eyes starting to water.

I turn and head towards the door, trying not to let the tears spill out, but there are some things that I cannot control. I can feel the wetness running down my cheeks when I reach the door, turning the handle.

I start to pull the door open when a hand is suddenly above my head, slamming the door closed. I turn my head, and I give G a questioning look. He stares back at me with a pained expression.

Seeing my tears, he cups my face with his hands and gently wipes them away with his thumbs. His touch helps me relax into his hands, but at the same time, I wish the situation was different.

Staring deep into my eyes, G leans forward, lightly brushing his lips against mine. When he doesn't feel me tense up or pull away, he pulls me into his chest and deepens the kiss. *I can't do this anymore!*

I push G away, breaking the kiss. My sadness from G's revelation turns into confused anger. "What do you want from me G?" I snap. "You make it perfectly clear that you don't want me, and that you being tied to me is causing you anguish. In less than a second, you are gentle and passionate with me and in the next second blaming and hurting me! All you have been doing to me is confusing me and kicking me in the chest, and I'm tired of it!" I'm yelling now. "I can't keep playing this emotional mind fuck you got going and having me as an unwilling participant!"

I decided to see if I can break whatever bond I have with G. I reach down inside myself, finding that well of power, looking for the energy to break the tie. Finding the energy, I keep drawing more and more power to search that invisible tether between G and I. Finding the chord, I use more power, trying very hard to break it.

Funny thing about titanium rings, if one gets stuck on your finger, you need a diamond cutter to remove the ring. I don't have the proverbial "diamond cutter" to cut this fucking bond. It feels like I'm trying to cut through titanium with a butter knife. I'm not strong enough yet in my body to use the energy needed to break the bond. I should have heeded G's words about powerful energy requiring a strong body. I stop calling on my power, feeling drained.

There is something wet running down my nose. My hand comes back with bright red blood from wiping at the wetness. I'm suddenly feeling extremely lightheaded and black spots start to blur my vision before I feel myself collapsing; watching the floor rushing up to meet me.

CHAPTER 9

Please Enjoy Your Visit to Hell

I start coming to, hearing a loud voice. "What the fuck did you say to her?" It was Virgil, and he sounds pissed.

"That I wanted to be free," G muttered.

"I never took you for a coward Gabriel. That 'little girl' you mockingly call her almost fucking died trying to give YOU your freedom. And now she's broken, which in turn breaks the rest of us." Virgil says.

I squeeze my eyes tighter, trying to block out the pain in my chest. "You better fucking fix this with her NOW GABRIEL!" And then I hear boots stomping away and a door slamming.

I open my eyes, looking around and notice I'm back in room number three. The ache in my body, as well as my soul, is tearing me apart. I slowly sit up, wanting more than anything to pass out and forget. But I still have a mission to complete. Always moving forward, take the good with the bad.

I stand up, realizing I'm still in my crimson bathrobe. I walk over to my backpack and notice that it's half empty with no clothes. I walk over to the closet, sliding open the door, and see all my clothes and undergarments neatly organized and folded. A small grin appears on my lips. Virgil is sweet.

I hear a door softly close behind me. I turn around, and there is G. He looks like shit. Like he hasn't slept or showered for days. His usually glowing green eyes are dull. Like something died in him. He can't even look into my eyes. I just stare, waiting for him to say something.

The waiting and silence start to become increasingly uncomfortable. G finally stutters "Sera, I'm truly sorry. I would never have thought or believed that you would try to break a soul bond."

I shrug, "You wanted to be free." I say calmly.

"And I regret about blaming the situation on you. I haven't regretted my actions in a very, very long time. But I regret the way I've been treating you. I never wanted for you to even try something suicidal like an attempt to free me. When I felt you trying to sever the bond, I felt like I was being torn apart," he admits.

I started approaching him softly until I was half a foot away from him. "What do you want?" I whisper.

"You," G groans, grabbing me by my shoulders and pulling me to him, crushing his lips into mine. I'm so overwhelmed by emotions, that tears spill down my face. I sigh and part my lips so he can assault me with his tongue. I feel myself getting wet, wanting and needing him.

He grabs my ass and lifts me up so I can wrap my legs around his waist. By the feel of his massive cock through his pants, he was more than ready to go. So was I. Holding me he walks forward, so my back hits the wall.

Without breaking our kiss, he uses the wall as leverage to lift me so he can unbutton his pants, releasing his cock. And still, with the one hand, he gently reaches in between my legs, feeling how dripping wet my pussy is. He stops kissing me. "Fuck, you're sopping wet," he says. "I'm going to fix that."

And with that, he guides his massive cock to my entrance and impales me. He starts thrusting into me with a frenzy. "Oh god Sera!" G exclaims. I felt like my heart was melting.

He then uses his thumb to rub my clit, causing a sudden orgasm to rip down my body, causing me to clutch onto G like a life raft. And my pussy refuses to stop milking his cock. "Fuck!" I yell. "I can't stop coming!" G just looks into my eyes with a smile on his face, pounding into me.

I then notice that his green eyes are starting to glow. And then his missing wings spring out. Except they are not the original black leathery wings, I saw when I first met him. The wings are now feathered, but still black. And they are fucking beautiful. I reach out and touch his wing. He closes his eyes and shudders. *The dark angel likes that hmmm?*

He keeps pounding into me, bringing out another orgasm except bigger and he comes with me, growling his release, shooting his cum into my pussy. When the orgasm hits, I see a blinding light and feel my heart swell a little.

When I open my eyes, G is staring at me wide-eyed and breathing heavy. He then puts his forehead to mine. "You will be the death of me little girl," he says.

"Promise?" I tease with a grin and kiss him on the lips.

G pulls out of me and puts me down gently. I hear a slight cough, and I turn my head to see Virgil leaning against the open door frame. He has an expression of relief on his face. "We make up?" he asks.

I give Virgil a shy smile, but G surprises me by putting his arm around my chest, and pulling my back to him, actually holding me. I feel relaxed and comfortable leaning into him. I then see Virgil smiling. *Definitely need to clear up some things.*

I step out of G's embrace and walk between both men. "G and Virgil," I begin. "I am equally attracted to both of you and want to be with both of you. If you don't want to share me and rather stay away, I completely understand." I twist my head to G to see how he is handling my announcement.

G is still smiling and says, "I don't mind sharing. Virgil?"

"Not at all," Virgil says. "But," Virgil continues. "It has to be equal."

"Okay, equal," I say, happily agreeing.

Walking over to the bed and sitting at the edge, I say, "I have a few questions, and if both of you don't want to answer, it's okay. No pressure." I close my eyes, take a deep breath and turn to G.

"G, why did your wings look like leather when I first met you, and why do they now have feathers?" I can see that G was uncomfortable with my questions but closes and opens his eyes, also taking in a deep breath, and walks over to sit next to me on the bed.

"Remember when Virgil mentioned the Fall, and I also mentioned that I was an archangel general?" I nodded my head. G continues. "The Fall started several millennia ago when Lucifer wanted to give humans the gift of unrestrained free will. Making humans no better than monkeys."

Interrupting G, I ask, "What do mean 'unrestrained' free will?"

"Humans would have no conscious or morals." G explains.

"How would Lucifer have been able to do that?" I ask.

"Do you know the seven deadly sins?" G asks. I give G a hesitant nod.

I did see the movie Seven, but that was years ago. Too dark and sad for me to watch except for a handful of times. "From what I can remember there is: Wrath, Sloth, Lust, and Envy," I say.

G nods and finishes with "Greed, Gluttony, and Pride. When The Creator sent us down, the seven archangels, we were the embodiment of the seven heavenly virtues: Forgiveness, Chastity, Temperance, Charity, Diligence, Kindness, and Humility. I was Forgiveness."

I take his hand into mine and ask softly, "What happened?"

G sighs. "We were fighting Lucifer and the fallen angels for centuries. Inadvertently wreaking destruction and death on humans. All major catastrophes in the early human record were because of the war." He rubs a hand through is onyx hair, recalling painful memories. "All those souls, all of them sent to Lucifer because the idea of The Creator was lost on many but to a very few. Why the early writings describe The Creator as vengeful. The Creator was pissed about Lucifer's disobedience, so any unbelieving human killed as a casualty of the war was automatically sent to Lucifer, pissing me the fuck off in the process. I was the embodiment of Forgiveness. Where was that Forgiveness for those poor souls? The more humans killed, the angrier I got until I disobeyed and turned into Wrath. When that happened, I physically transformed into a black dragon."

"Hence the leather looking wings," I said, feeling there is more to his story of his turning into a pissed off dragon, but I let it go for now. G nods his head and continues.

"I couldn't return to my angelic form, so for many centuries I lived in isolation in Northern England; until the human population exploded and reached my isolated area." He closed his eyes and smirked. "I really enjoyed scaring the shit out of the humans, but they decided to hire a knight to hunt and kill me. The bastard was relentless, but I didn't know the knight was gifted with a holy sword. So one day I decided to kill him, getting tired of him pursuing me. I set a trap for him, but that mother fucker was cunning." There was no resentment in his voice, only admiration. "He got the drop on me, and before I knew it, I got stabbed by the holy sword; however, I inadvertently killed the knight in the process. The sword did not kill me, but transformed my appearance to a human, resembling the fallen knight, except with dragon wings. I took the sword, learned how to hide my wings, and headed back to the village that hired the knight. It was there I learned that the knight's name was George, and I wandered the country, telling tales about George the Dragon Slayer. A pope got wind of the tale, and George was sainted. The rest is history as they say." G said with a shrug. *Damn!*

"So, because of you Sera, showing me what Forgiveness was again by nearly sacrificing your life in your attempt to free me after how I treated you. I was able to learn what forgiveness meant, and balance the wrath in me. Hence turning my wings into feathers once more. But as a reminder of my disobedience, they are black," he finished.

"So the sword was Cal?" I asked.

"Cal?" G asks.

"Oh, that's my nickname for it; it likes the nickname. Excalibur I mean." I tell him.

"What do you mean 'it likes' the name Cal?" G says looking at me quizzically.

"The sword talks to me. Didn't it talk to you?" I ask G.

"Not a fucking peep," responds G, his face still has an expression of awe on it.

"Oh," I respond with a shrug. Moving on.

I turn to Virgil, who is still leaning against the master bedroom door frame. "What about you Virgil?" I politely ask. "You are not one of the seven archangels, so why do you need to be saved?"

Virgil walks over to the bed and sits next to me, opposite of G. "Well," he says. "I was an ancient philosopher, and I also taught that to reach inner peace, one must accept The Love Element."

I interrupted Virgil asking, "The 'Love Element'?".

"Yes," Virgil replies, "I believe that there are more than the four elements that humans can feel besides the physical."

"More than earth, air, fire, and water?" I ask.

"Yes," Virgil responds, "I believe in three extra elements called: Light, Spirit, and Love. Those three elements are potent and important for a human to gain inner peace." Okay, sounds logical.

"But," Virgil states, looking sad, "The leaders of the city dismissed The Love Element, calling it a woman's weakness. I refused to stop teaching Love as an element and was labeled as a heretic. I was tried and found guilty by my peers, sentenced to drink hemlock." *Shit.*

"Why weren't you sent to Heaven?" I ask.

"I was raised to believe in many gods. So I was placed in Limbo with the unbelievers," Virgil states.

"Why were you chosen for this mission?" I inquire.

Virgil sighs, "Because even though I was punished by the city leaders and in essence martyred, I never once stopped believing in my teachings. Even through the centuries when I was wandering through Limbo, I never let my beliefs go. I guess The Creator decided I was pure enough to earn my redemption by guiding you through Hell." Virgil finishes.

I grab his hands with mine and look into those beautiful swirling pools of silver. I give him a brief kiss. "I'm glad you were picked," I tell him with a smile.

G cuts in, saying, "We should get some rest. Tomorrow we arrive at the First Circle." I turn to him, frowning. "I thought this was a seven-day trip? It's only been two days," I say. Virgil clears his throat, making me turn my head back to him.

"You were passed out for four days. You almost died using the powerful energy it took in your attempt to break the soul bond with G. You needed to rest to re-energize," Virgil explains.

"Okay," I say, looking down at the comforter suddenly feeling timid and vulnerable. "Will both of you stay here and sleep with me?" I quietly ask.

I then feel strong arms pull me across the sheets, to the head of the bed, letting me lay down and placing the covers on top of me. I then see both G and Virgil undress, both commando by the way. *A magnificent sight!*

They both slip into the bed on either side of me, placing their strong arms on me, making me safe and at peace. My eyes get heavy, and I drifted off to sleep.

I wake with a slow realization that I have two gorgeous men sleeping on either side of me. And both have morning wood. *What to do?*

I'm feeling a little naughty and place both hands on each erect cock; playfully stoking each in a steady rhythm. G was the first to grab my shoulder and roll me to the side to face him.

I still have my hand on Virgil's cock, but I feel him scoot closer to where he's spooning me. "Someone wants to play," G matter of factually states.

"Who me?" I flirtatiously say. "I was just trying to wake you both up. I guess you don't like how I did it." I stop stroking G.

He stares at me with glowing green eyes filled with lust and want. He then looks over my shoulder to Virgil. "Want to show her that it's not nice to tease?" he asks Virgil.

"I'm up for it," responds Virgil. I snort at the pun Virgil said, trying not to show my amusement. I'm going to have much fun with these two.

I'm still in the red crimson robe, so G tugs on the bow knot that was keeping the robe closed. With the knot undone, G pushes the robe open revealing my breasts, nipples already hard, begging to be played with. G lowers his head, taking a nipple into his mouth. Shit!

I'm getting wet with need. I'm still stroking Virgil's cock, and I resume stroking G's cock.

I feel Virgil's hand sliding to the front of me, heading down to my aching pussy. He slowly rubs his finger in my wet folds, circling my wetness around my pussy, but ignoring my clit. I groan in frustration. I hear Virgil chuckle "Not done teasing you yet baby," he whispers. Oh, fuck me!

I then feel Virgil spreading my ass cheeks, using my wetness to insert a finger into the other hole. He keeps switching from front to back until he gets two fingers in. Meanwhile, G is still sucking on my tits, helping me relax to Virgil's playful administration to my ass. I then feel three fingers, sliding in and out of me. Shit! That is starting to feel good.

G stops sucking the tit he was on, looks over my shoulder to Virgil and nods. I'm suddenly lifted up like I weigh nothing, and G scoots underneath me, letting me straddle him with his cock at my entrance. G slides into my wet pussy, filling me up, holding my waist with his hands.

He starts rocking his hips into me while drawing me forward so my ass is in the air and I'm practically laying on his massive chest. I then feel Virgil sticking his three fingers into my asshole, rubbing my wetness into me, lubing me up. I have a feeling I know what's going to happen next, and frankly, I can't fucking wait!

I then feel Virgil's breath at my ear, "Are you going to be a good little girl and take both of us?" he whispers.

"Yes!" I hiss.

"Yes, what?" he teases. His fingers and G's cock stops thrusting into me. Now I feel like I'm going to cry in frustration because I need to release soon.

"Yes, Please!" I shout, putting the frustration into my voice.

"So be it," Virgil says.

Virgil removes his fingers, replacing them with the head of his cock. He starts to push in slowly, a new type of fullness invading my lust filled haze. He slowly thrusts in and out, forcing a little further in each time. G slowly starts to shove in me, helping me relax so Virgil can get his cock all the way into my ass.

I'm bordering pain and pleasure because I feel so stretched and full. Virgil reaches a hand around me while G is thrusting into me, his fingers finally on my clit, massaging it until I can feel that pressure is building up again. Virgil then starts moving slowly. Holy Shit! "Oh Fuck!" I yell. "Come for us, baby!" G growls.

When I do come, I roar because the sensation is so intense. I feel like I blacked out for a second, but then I feel both G and Virgil both pounding into me. "Oh My God!" I scream as orgasm number two hits me like a fucking wrecking ball. But the guys are not done yet.

I look down at G and notice that his beautiful raven black wings have popped out. He must be loving this as much as me. Both men really start to hammer my pussy and ass because I feel a massive orgasm coming on like no other. "I'm going to explode! Don't stop fucking me!" I demand.

"Milk our cocks baby girl," Virgil says. And I comply with his command.

My pussy is clenching tightly around G's cock, forcing my ass to grip Virgil's cock as well, causing both men to shout their release. This time when I close my eyes, I see a blinding white light and a feeling of euphoria that I have never known.

"Holy shit!" I hear Virgil yell, his seamen still squirting into my ass. I look behind me, seeing that my fiery wings have come out. I hope they are not burning Virgil.

"Damn, little girl," G says. "You are definitely a hot little piece aren't you?" he says with a grin. I turn my head and grin back.

"You know it so don't ever forget it," I teasingly quip. It's then I saw a hint of sadness in G's eyes. It was so fast I almost missed it, G quickly hiding the look with amusement.

I hear Virgil chuckling. I turn my head back. My wings disappeared again. "You okay?" I ask Virgil with a concerned voice. He smiles at me.

"You didn't burn me," he assuringly says. "Your wings exploding out of your back like that surprised me." Virgil then gently pulls his cock out of my ass. I lean back and give him a peck on the lips.

I then turn back to G and also gave him a small kiss. I lift myself up, his cock coming out of me. "Shower time," I say sweetly to my men.

"Lead the way," G says.

Taking a shower with my two guys was a revelation. Every crack and crevice on my body was cleaned; everything was touched and massaged with care. I, of course, got to perform the same task on both my men, letting me fully explore their bodies.

After the shower, we got dressed and packed our bags. When we step into the main room, an even more massive buffet was set up, with every brunch item you can think of.

Since I haven't eaten for five days and had a lot of sex in between, I hurriedly grabbed a plate and started loading it with eggs, pancakes, cheeses, fruits, different sandwiches, and other items until I couldn't fit anything else. I quickly sat down at the dining table and started stuffing my face with gusto.

When my plate is nearly empty, I stop and realize that I'm the only one sitting and eating. I look at the location where I left my guys, and both were staring at me in amazement. "What?" I ask them. "I'm hungry," I say with a shrug.

G turns to Virgil and says "She makes more groans of pleasure when eating than when she had both our cocks in her, making her orgasm so hard her wings popped out." Virgil snorts and starts laughing, nodding in agreement. I roll my eyes at them. *Boys.*

I clear my plate and get up to grab another plate to load up with the foods I was unable to fit on my first plate. I turn back to the guys, both grinning at me. "Are you going to eat?" I ask them.

"Is there any food left for us?" asks Virgil.

"Eat me," I tell him.

"Tempting, really tempting but we are close to arriving at the First Circle," Virgil replies. I just shake my head and return to my seat.

I begin eating much slower, savoring the food this time. I hear the sound of plates and utensils used for scooping food onto the plates. The guys place their dishes on each side of me, each taking their seat to the left and right of me. Feels like a family meal I muse.

Then I remember the meals I had with my adopted parents, feeling sad that nothing would ever be the same again. I take a deep breath. "Penny for your thoughts?" Virgil asks. That's why I love him so much. Always caring about my feelings.

"Was remembering meal times with my parents," I say. G grabs my hand and gives it a squeeze. Virgil leans into me, giving me a soft kiss on the cheek. Both actions lifting my spirits and makes me smile at both of them. "Thank you," I say.

There's a knock at the door. G gets up and answers it. Charon strolls in, looking like the playmate of the year. "We have arrived," she says quietly to us.

I give her a friendly smile, and say "Thank you." She actually gives me a warm smile in return.

"You're welcome," she replies and turns to the door, leaving the room.

"I wonder why she's nice to me? Especially since she couldn't have sex with either of you?" asking no one in particular. Virgil looks down at his plate, blushing slightly.

"What?" I ask.

"This boat is Charon's floating harem," G explains. "Any soul she is attracted to, she keeps for herself. She never has a dry spell when it comes to sex."

A thought pops into my head, "Do her lovers row the boat?"

"Yes, four men to an oar, plus any other manual labor she needs to keep this boat going," G says. *Busy girl!*

We quickly finish eating, collect our belongings, strapping Cal to my back and putting on the backpack. We all head out the door and are blinded by sunshine. Bright, beautiful sunlight.

We all walk across the deck, the sunlight shining down in a clear blue sky. So blue in fact that it couldn't be real. We head to the gangplank, stepping on and walking down to a well-constructed dock. Once I am on the pier, I am able to take in the scene around me. It's beautiful here. So beautiful that it seems wrong.

CHAPTER 10

First Circle, Lust Land

I see a never-ending, crystal blue sky, without a cloud to mar the perfection. The picturesque ceiling ends miles away, with the start of a sea of blue-green grass that looks like soft, shaggy carpet. The grass meets at us at the end of pier, with a dirt road that cuts through the eternal, grassy sea.

"Welcome to the first section of the divine sewage system," says Virgil.

"What happens here?" I ask.

"This is the place where those who practiced the deadly sin of Lust in life receive their eternal punishment."

"Doesn't everyone suffer from lust every now and then?" I ask him.

"There are those who start a relationship with lust but make and keep an oath to be true to that relationship; whereas there are those who make false oaths, fornicating with anyone that they have a mutual attraction with," Virgil explains.

"Like my promise to stay faithful to both of you and the six others that I have to save and your promise to be forever mine?" I say.

"Exactly," Virgil replies.

Looking towards G, I catch that same fleeting, sad look, quickly hidden when he feels my eyes on him. He suddenly grins at me, and I return the grin.

"Ready?" I ask G.

"Ready," G answers with the confidence I wish I had.

We walk across the dock, stepping onto a dirt path heading towards an endless, green horizon. We start walking down the path, heading away from the pier. We walk by beautiful meadows housing flowers with bright, dazzling colors that could never exist on Earth. But it still feels wrong to me.

Feeling like a couple of hours have passed, the sunlight remains the same, bright and overhead like it's midday.

After many miles, the path suddenly stops, turning into a ledge because there is an almost vertical drop in the landscape. An extremely steep set of stairs winds down the side of what look likes an endless hill with no bottom. I can't even see the base of the stairs; they keep going down. I whistle. "Fuck," I state.

It was then that I heard it. A sound like a wind tunnel being turned on followed by roar of painful screaming. Thousands of screaming voices coming from below, heading our way.

In the distance, I see what looks like garbage being blown up the hill. It takes a minute until I can discern that the trash is, in fact, a vast mass of human bodies flung around in a tornado being pushed up the hill.

When the mass of the hundreds of thousands to even millions of bodies nearly reaches us at the top, the wind stops, plummeting the mass down the hill. Bouncing, screaming, naked bodies going all over the place as they drop.

"Since they went wherever the wind blew them in life, the same happens to them in their afterlife, literally," Virgil says.

My God! "Is there a faster way down?" I ask either of the guys.

"I can float us down with my wings," G volunteers.

"Sounds good to me," says Virgil.

I swallow, forcing my head to nod in agreement. I'm not a fan of heights.

G is holding me tight on one side of his body, Virgil on the other side of him. He releases those magnificent black wings, spreading them out at least ten feet each way. He jumps off the edge of the path, and I feel in that brief moment my stomach jumping into my throat.

I think G and Virgil are aware of my discomfort because G looks at me and smiles reassuringly, hugging me close to his body. Virgil reaches over and cups my face, also giving me a smile.

We descend and keep on dropping. The high noon sunlight always the same intensity. I don't remember how many times we saw the mass of bodies tumbling up and down the hill, the screams announcing their imminent passing. Poor souls.

I look up to G, seeing that he's sweating with a look of strain on his face. I look down, and still, there is no end in sight. "G," I say softly, "I know you need to rest. Tuck your wings in and let us fall. When you see the ground, float us down. We still don't know how far the ground is."

G closes his eyes and then looks at Virgil. Virgil nods in consent.

Even when you know that the drop of a roller coaster is about to happen, you are always unprepared for that jolt and that sudden feeling of falling. And fall we did. G keeps Virgil and me tight in his arms. It takes a few seconds for our bodies to get adjusted to the speed of the fall. I still see no ground in sight.

"G, since we are in the Land of the Lust, does that mean one your comrades is here?" I ask him.

"Yes," he replies.

"Which one?" I ask.

He shrugs and shakes his head. "I don't know," G says, "but we will definitely find out."

I sigh. "One more question, G." He turns his beautiful face towards me. "How do I save someone who now is the embodiment of Lust?"

He turns his head forward, a small grin appearing on his face. I feel my cheeks flush. *Worry about it later.*

After hours of falling, I drift to sleep due to boredom, something I wouldn't imagine to be possible under the circumstances. And then I am jolted awake, looking up at G, seeing his wings are out. I look down and sigh with relief. *There is a ground!*

We float down and land on soft blue-green grass. Still a beautiful sunny day. Probably another reason why this is Hell. I've heard that people go batshit crazy when the lights are on all day, every day because they cannot tell if it's day or night, no way to determine time.

Speaking of batshit crazy, here comes the screaming mass of bodies tumbling down the insane hill. And then the invisible wind tunnel turns on to push those poor souls back up the hill.

"Which way Virgil?" I ask.

"I don't know," he responds.

I snap my head to him, a question on my face.

"You have to feel for that energy that makes us unique," G says. I reach out, feeling G's and Virgil's energy signatures. I then reach further and further out, not feeling anything. I keep going and there! The signature is very weak, so weak that I almost missed it. I look at G and Virgil and point to the horizon.

"That way," I direct, seeing an endless sea of green in every direction in front of us.

We start walking in the direction I pointed to, my guys on either side of me. The grass is crunching under my boots. I look around and notice no trees, nothing to indicate some kind of shade. No wind or clouds to give us relief from unrelenting sunlight but with no sun in the sky. Where is the heat coming from?

To conserve energy, talking is kept to a minimum. We continue on, walking, mile after mile, hour after hour. I randomly check the energy signature, feeling us getting a little closer to it.

"We need to rest for a bit," Virgil says.

I nod in agreement and stop to take off my pack. G and Virgil do the same.

G starts rummaging through his bag and produces large, wrapped protein bars and a large bottle of water to share. I take a bar, remove the wrapper, and start chewing. I don't care about the taste since I'm hungry and take a swig of water. My stomach starts to feel somewhat content.

"We will sleep in shifts," G states. "One will watch while the other two sleep."

"I volunteer to take the first shift to watch," I offer. "Since I was able to get a few hours of sleep when we were falling for almost forever." Both men look at me, seeing if I was fine to take the first watch. "Seriously guys," I say, lifting my chin in challenge, "I'm good to go."

G nods "Okay, Sera," he says, "you get the first watch, but you better wake one of us up when you start feeling tired."

I stand at attention and perform a military salute, "Yes, sir!" I say with a grin.

"Smart ass," G says. I just smile, feeling happy that G is starting to show his confidence in me.

Both guys unroll their sleeping bags, climb in and use the backpacks to shade themselves against the never-ending sunlight. I sit and just watch my surroundings for about an hour until I get restless.

Deciding to practice my magic, I get up, wondering if I can tap into any other elements. "Cal?" I say in my head.

"Yes, little one?" is the reply.

"Am I able to create or use the other physical elements?" I ask.

"Yes, even the non-physical elements."

Okay then. I take a deep, calming breath and find that deep well of energy in me. I think of the fuels needed to create fire: earth, air, and heat. But I know that pure oxygen is exceptionally combustible, so technically I only need air and heat. *Chemistry 101, baby!*

I then get an idea. Like with the air training session with G (aka "G getting his ass kicked!") I mold the air. Except this time, I focus on the mold itself, finding the energy signatures of the molecules down to each atom.

I separate the bonds of the carbon and oxygen atoms, the ripping of the bonds creating heat. I open my eyes, and I have a small fireball the size of a grapefruit floating in midair. The shock of my success startles me, I lose focus and cause the ball to extinguish. Trying again, I create fire much faster since I know what I'm looking for. I'm feeling elated because I just created fire out of thin air!

I practice for a couple of hours until the feeling of tiredness starts creeping into my body. I return to our camp and reach over to sleeping Virgil with the intent to slightly shake his leg, when the sky goes suddenly pitch black. *Oh no!*

A feeling of trepidation overcomes me.

The blackness is so thick that I cannot see my hand one inch in front of my eyes. I feel for Virgil's leg and start shaking him awake wildly. "G, Virgil!" I exclaim. "We have a huge fucking problem!"

I use my "third eye" to "see" the guys' distinct energy signatures, and their glowing eyes lets me know which way they are facing. And then I feel other energy signatures out in the blackness. There is no way to describe this signature except that if evil had a signature, it would look like the ones swarming towards us. "We got company!" I yell. "Coming from every direction!"

I turn my back to the guys, stepping backward closer to them to form a defensive perimeter. I am fighting down the panic that wants me to tuck tale and run screaming as far away from here as possible. Focusing, I pull Cal out. "Cal? What is coming this way?"

"Succubi" Cal says.

"What are Succubi?" I ask out loud to the guys.

"Oh, fuck!" G groans. "Those little fuckers are vicious! Sucking dry anything with sexual energy. Little fucking parasites."

Seeing the energy signatures from the Succubi closing in and surrounding us, I get an idea. "G," I say. "Let's slip into the stream and hack those little shits to pieces."

"Solid plan," G says. "You take the left, and I'll take the right. Virgil, kill any that breaks through."

Come to think of it, I've never seen Virgil use a weapon before. From Virgil's energy signature, I can see that he pulls out some sort of weapon. Then it starts to glow. It looks like a bow staff, but G sounded confident of Virgil's fighting abilities, so I don't question the weapon he chooses.

Cal sensing my need for a glowing weapon, starts to illuminate a brilliant white light, bright enough for me to see ten feet all around me. I'm starting to feel confident as I slip into the stream.

In my first assault against the Succubi, I learn that the Succubi are fast, stupid, and hate light. When they see me coming like a white laser, the avant-garde immediately turns around and tries running back to where they came from, getting trampled by those behind them.

It's a major cluster fuck but making it extremely easy for me to slice Cal through their short bodies, like a hot knife through butter. I meet G halfway and turn around for another round of slicing. We must have killed thousands in about an hour. It seems that the little fuckers in the rear decide to retreat because I see their energy signatures speeding away from us until there is nothing. And then light instantly returns to the sky.

I have to shield my eyes, adjusting to the brightness. Eyes fixed, I see a field of carnage circling us. Looking closely at the bodies, the Succubi look like fucking Gremlins with razor sharp teeth and claws. And like Gremlins, their bodies slowly turn into ash in the light, the ground quickly soaking up the ash until the whole area is green grass again.

I walk back to our makeshift campsite, sheathing Cal, seeing G got there before me. Both the guys look fine except for the purple blood splattered all over them. And then I realize I'm covered in the purple shit too.

"You okay?" Virgil asks me.

"I'm good," I reply.

"Lucifer is testing us," G says.

"When I see Lucifer, I'm putting my size nine boot up his ass!" I say determinedly. I get a chuckle from the guys.

G rummages through his bag and hands me a pack of baby wipes. Damn! He's well prepared. I take a couple and pass the packet to Virgil. I wipe down my face and hands, taking off as much purple goo as I can.

Virgil looks at me "You and G rest for a few hours. I'll take watch."

I nod in agreement, " Thank you, Virgil," I tell him.

I unroll my sleeping bag, slip into it, not caring that my clothes are disgusting. Exhaustion hits me hard, and I'm out when my head hits the ground.

I must have slept for hours because I wake up ravenously hungry. Both guys are awake. I sit up and grab my bag, feeling in the front pocket. *Got it!* I grab a protein bar and rip it open as fast as I can. I start chowing down, and then I see the guys staring. "Oh!" I say with a mouth full of a bar. "You both want a bar?"

"No, thanks," are the replies I get.

I finish the bar and search my bag for water. I find the bottle and take a deep drink. Not knowing how much further we have until we reach the energy signatures for the door and Archangel, I put the rest of the bottle away.

I roll up my sleeping bag, reattach it to the backpack, and wait for the guys to get ready to leave. Both still staring at me, watching me intently. It's then that I notice the lust in their eyes. *This place is getting to them. Well, a roll in the grass couldn't hurt.*

I smile flirtatiously at both of them and then stand up because I'm going to play a little hard to get. Both men still staring at me, like predators hunting their prey. "Whoever catches me first without slipping into the stream gets to fuck me first!" And with that I turn and start sprinting away, laughing.

I make it to a quarter of a mile when hands grab my waist, turning me around and brutally kissing me. I'm wet, loving the feel of being dominated. From the taste of his lips, I know it is Virgil. Note to self, Virgil is faster than G, but not by much since G's there in less than a second.

G pulls me away from Virgil, also bruising my lips. Virgil is kissing my neck, and he then starts to rip my clothes off. Literally. I don't give a shit at this point, I'm too fucking wet with need.

G stops kissing me and then gently picks me up and lays me down. Virgil has gotten my shirt and bra off, breasts exposed, and is now working on my boots.

G decides to assault my breasts with vigor, taking a nipple in between his teeth, lightly nipping it, a groan escaping my lips, my pussy becoming wetter.

I then feel Virgil opening my web belt and tearing off my pants, not bothering with buttons. The buttons end up flying off from how hard he pulled the pants down my legs. Virgil then rips off my panties like they were tissue paper and places his mouth on my clit. *Fuck!*

He's sucking and licking the nub like it was the tip of an ice cream cone. The way that both men are aggressively pleasing my body makes me orgasm within seconds, causing me to shout out my pleasure, my pussy pulsing.

Virgil doesn't even bother to remove his pants. He undoes his pants button far enough for his huge, throbbing cock to come out. With my pussy still clenching, he thrusts himself into me. Fucking me like his life depends on it.

I'm loving the rough play until I see the pain in his eyes. Like he has no control over how hard he's fucking me. I pull his face down towards me, kissing his lips, trying to show that I'm enjoying his rough administration to my pussy. He looks down at me and keeps bucking his hips deep into me. I look over and see G stroking himself, waiting for his turn.

I come again, hard, screaming Virgil's name. Because of how hard he is fucking me, he comes in me with a yell, slowing down his thrusts and the wild lust gone from his eyes. One down, one more to go.

Virgil carefully removes himself from between my legs. I look over to G. "Your turn, big boy," I say flirtatiously.

"On your hands and knees," G commands. I'm ready to go again, enjoying being dominated. I roll over, spreading my legs and bending my arms a little to fully expose my pussy.

I see him walk over until he's behind me. He grabs my hips and holds me until he skewers me with his cock, thrusting into me like a wild animal.

I feel glorious! Enjoying the fast and hard pounding my pussy is receiving. I feel the pressure building. "Holy shit!" I groan.

"That's it, baby, take it like the good little girl you are," G says.

I come undone, saying G's name like a prayer. He also comes with a growl, shooting his warm cum into me.

He then collapses onto me, breathing on the back of my neck, then moving up to kiss my cheek. He pulls out of me and gingerly picks me up like a baby, carrying me back to the camp, Virgil walking next to us with only my boots and web belt in his hand. My shredded clothes are left in the grass.

G lays me softly on his sleeping bag, getting the baby wipes from his bag. Both men carefully wipe me down from head to toe, treating me with great reverence.

Virgil goes into my bag and retrieves a full change of clothes with underwear and another sports bra. When G is finally satisfied with how clean I am, he lets me get dressed. I feel fantastic about the whole experience, hoping we can do that again.

I finish dressing and look at both my guys, smiling. Both have frowns on their faces, not wanting to meet my eyes. *Uh?*

"What's the matter with you two? Did I do something wrong?" I ask. Both men look up at me with shock on their faces. "What?" I ask.

"You're not mad at us?" Virgil asks.

"Why would I be mad?"

"Because we were really rough with you," responds G.

Seriously?! "I actually enjoyed the hard sex. It was exciting, and I hope we do it again," I sincerely tell them. They were definitely not expecting that type of response from me.

"Come here, you two," I command. Both men come over and stop in front of me. I first walk up to Virgil, giving him a hot kiss which he happily returns, and then I do the same with G. Equal, remember?

"I would definitely let both of you know if the sex got too rough for my liking. Now that everything is great again, let's get going."

"Yes, ma'am!" both my guys say in unison. I'm a fortunate girl!

We start walking. And walking. Have I mentioned that Hell sucks? Mile after mile, hour after hour, we keep going, only taking short breaks. We need to get out of this circle of Hell as fast as possible, avoiding any more obstacles Lucifer might get an itch to throw at us.

Thank God the Succubi are the only nasty things Lucifer has sent our way so far, but I have a feeling we are pawns on his big chess board. Something isn't right, my gut is telling me.

At our next rest stop, looking at the guys, I say, "I have a feeling that Lucifer is fucking with us somehow." G and Virgil both nod in agreement. "The energy signature is slightly getting stronger, but when I initially felt it back at the hill, it didn't seem this far away."

Virgil, scrunching his face, says, "Lucifer is mighty and can distort space, making it seem like it can go on forever."

A thought hits me. "Virgil, you said when we got off the ship that this was the first part of Hell's sewage system. What if this circle is like a big toilet bowl and we are going around and around in a huge circle? Never meant to reach the middle where the door is?"

He scratches his chin in thought. "It's possible, but we need to test that theory somehow."

I cock my head and I look at G. Do we have something that we can roll or use a leveler? This place looks flat, but if we are supposed to go 'down,' a ball or something can show us the actual tilt of the landscape."

G goes into his pack, pulls out a giant roll of duct tape.

"Always have duct tape on hand," he says with a wink.

Standing up, I unravel the tape to about two feet, letting the roll swing until it stops. I lower it to the ground. "Virgil, do you see any tilt to the landscape compared to the roll?"

Virgil gets on his hands and knees. "Well, I'll be damned! There is a tilt to the land," he says, pointing to his left."And a decent pitch too." Looking up at me he asks, "How did you know that would work?"

I shrug, responding, "I watched a documentary about gravity and the theory that gravity is relative to space and time. We have no time here, and space is made to look infinite, but it's really not. We can't feel the effects of the tilt, meaning that this place is somehow moving. So that leaves the laws of gravity. I assumed that Lucifer cannot break the laws, and therefore I used the weight of the tape roll to see which way gravity is pulling down."

Both men silently stare at me, a look of wonderment in their eyes. "Yes, I'm an encyclopedia of trivial information," I teasingly inform them.

"Definitely comes in handy," G says to no one in particular. I shrug my shoulders and smile.

I carefully roll the duct tape back up and hand the roll to G. "Let's get moving. Hopefully, this won't be a long walk."

It is another few hours until I see what looks like a white structure in the distance, and I feel an energy signature similar to the first gate we passed through when entering Hell.

"We are coming up to the gate," says G.

Thank God! I also feel that very faint energy signature coming from the direction of the structure.

The closer we get, the more massive the structure becomes. A couple of hours later, I'm seeing massive white walls, going miles in either direction.

Walking up to the wall, I look up to see where the building ends and the sky begins. I am overcome by the same feelings I had when I visited New York City.

I am in awe of the gigantic structure in front of me; making me feel puny and insignificant. I smirk and look at the guys. "Do you think Lucifer is overcompensating for something?"

Both G and Virgil smile at me. "Next question. How the fuck do we get in?" I ask. Both men shake their heads, unable to answer my question.

The white, gleaming wall reminds me how beautifully fucked up this place really is. Too perfect to be real. *I wonder?*

I stick my hand out to see what the texture feels like. My hand goes through the wall! I turn and look at the guys. "We should all step through together," I suggest. "Lucifer may have a stupid trick up his sleeve."

Virgil nods. "I agree. How about you, G?" G also nods, and both men step up to stand on each side of me. I take both their hands, and we walk through the wall.

And walking into a dark, dank corridor that has no end in sight. I drop the guys' hands and turn around to see if we can leave just in case. My hand hits a solid wall. The only way to go is forward.

We start walking forward, noting open doorways to the left and right of us, each leading down another corridor that twists and turns. "Looks like we are in a huge labyrinth," I surmise.

"Fucking Lucifer and his stupid childish games," G says with an angry growl.

I then have another thought. "I hope it's just us in here and none of Lucifer's fucked up creations." Famous last words. Something in the distance roars.

"Shit," Virgil whispers.

My sentiments exactly!

I feel out for the gate and the dim energy signatures. "Guys, I feel that distinctive archangel energy signature in here, and it's moving."

"We need to collect the archangel that the energy belongs to. That's the mission," G states.

"Which way?" asks Virgil.

I point my finger at the wall. "That general direction," I state.

"Looks like we have to go down corridors," G says.

"We need something to mark the ground or walls to let us know we passed this way if we get lost or need to backtrack," I say.

"I can do that," says Cal in my head.

Pulling Cal out of the sheath, the sword starts glowing gold. I keep my focus on the moving energy while leading us to our first turn from the main corridor. I cut a deep groove into the corner of the wall, Cal leaving something in the slot that makes it glow gold.

"Works for me," G says.

I keep focusing on the moving energy signature, making slashes at each turn. Of course, we hit a couple of dead ends and have to backtrack.

I place a second slash in the corner to let us know that there's a dead end ahead. It felt like we were gaining on the moving energy source an inch an hour.

"We need to take a break," commands G. I nod in agreement. Too hungry and exhausted to say anything, we sit where we stop, able to see both ways down the corridor just in case the thing that roared wants us for a snack.

Sitting against the wall, I get as comfortable as I can. G gets more protein bars, passing them to Virgil and me. I quickly scarf the meal down.

"G," I say, turning to him, "when this little trip is over, I'm never eating another protein bar ever again." I made sure he was seeing my 'serious' face. He gives me a big smile. He's so fucking handsome when he smiles!

I lose my stern face and smile in return. Impulsively I lean over, kissing G on the cheek. That is not enough for him and so he pulls me into his arms for a tender but hot kiss. I sigh into his arm, content with kissing him in return.

A minute later we gently break apart. And then I turn to Virgil. *Equal remember?* Sidling up to Virgil, I wrap my arms around his neck and kiss him. Just like with G, our kiss is sweet and tender. Kissing these two men makes me happy. Even though we are sitting in a labyrinth, and the atmosphere is depressing as hell.

I could feel my eyes getting heavy. I am using a lot of energy to track the fallen archangel. Both my guys lean on either side of me, giving me their body heat, making me feel warm and cozy. I drift off to sleep.

I'm walking down dark corridors, a feeling of familiarity is calming me, like a sense de ja vu. I hear a loud roar, and it's incredibly close. But I'm not scared, the roar is full of pain and frustration. Don't ask me how I know that. I just do. I keep walking toward the sound, knowing that at the end of this corridor will be a generous bedroom.

Walking into the bedroom, every furnishing looks familiar. Whoever decorated this room has really gaudy tastes. Gold trim on the tops and bottoms of the crimson walls. Golden naked female statues placed in wall nooks around the room. The massive gold canopy bed covered in crimson satin sheets, bordered with gold.

But the room is not empty. A naked male with golden skin, beautiful red wings, and short golden hair has his back to me. "Hello?" I tentatively ask.

He turns around.

Oh my fucking God! He's extremely handsome. What's with angels and their unearthly beauty? His eyes are red, like his wings. He has a square jaw, a perfect nose, and totally kissable lips.

Heat surges through me. I can feel my nipples getting hard and my pussy getting wet. I haven't even looked at the rest of him yet. My eyes wander down his body. Yep, another perfectly sculpted body and a massive cock, already erect. I look back up to his eyes noting that he looks pained.

"Who are you?" I ask. As if to respond, he opens his mouth and a huge roar comes out. When he stops roaring, he gives me a look of pure anguish. I need to help him. His pain is tearing at my soul. He opens his mouth again, and I hear a mix of the roar with "Sera!" coming out.

What? That voice sounds like Virgil. "Sera! Wake up!" Shit.

Eyes snapping open, I stare into Virgil's panicked grey ones. I hear a roar to my left. I turn my head, and I see G, black wings out, black sword unsheathed, facing off with something huge. I stand up, drawing Cal and walking towards G, getting close enough to see what the hell G is about to fight.

Standing behind G to the side, I see what I can only describe as a Minotaur. A huge fucking Minotaur; a man's body with a huge bull's head on top. With red eyes. *Uh oh!*

"Cal?" I say in my head.

"Yes, little one?" Cal responds.

"I think we found our missing archangel. What do I have to do for him to get back to his natural form?" I ask.

"You have to stab him with me." Cal starts glowing red. Awesome.

"G," I say, placing my hand on the small of his back. "I have to fight him." He looks at me like I've lost my fucking mind. I guess I have but trying to explain my dream to him would sound even more fucked up.

Looking into his glowing green eyes, I say pleadingly, "Trust me. Please". G narrows his eyes at me, grinding his teeth.

"You fucking die and I'll follow you to Hell to get you back."

Did he just make a joke at this critical time?

I try not to crack a smile but what can I say? I have a dark sense of humor.

"Awww, you do like me," I tease. From the look he gives me, I'm not too sure if he wants to kiss me or pick me up and run for it. "I got this," I say with false bravado. I'm truly scared shitless.

I turn towards bull-man, ready to help the angel stuck inside there.

I'm walking towards the freakishly large man with a massive bull's head. And when I say freakishly large, I mean everywhere because bull-man has no qualms about being butt-ass naked.

I swallow hard, praying that when I get the bull-man back to his standard form, the monstrosity between his legs becomes human size.

Taking a deep breath, I slip into the stream. And then bull-man plucks me out of it. Before I can grasp how deep in shit I am, bull-man tosses me over his shoulder, turns around, and slips into the stream. At least he's cognitive enough not to kill me outright. Yet.

CHAPTER 11

TAKING THE BULL BY THE HORNS

After what feels like hours in the stream, because time moves differently, bull-man stops and unceremoniously dumps me onto a cushioned surface. I still have Cal in my hand. Thank God for small mercies! I definitely underestimated bull-man, assuming that he is dumb as a bull.

I sit up, looking the bull in the eyes, so to speak. Assessing my body movements, eyeing Cal warily, not sure if I'll use my sword. He's a good ten feet away from me. I'm also eyeing him, determining if he is going to gorge me to death or worse.

He slips into the stream. A good fucking thing I am prepared. I dig deep inside me and call air. Like with G, I fling a ball of air at him, and I miss! I slip into the stream, going ludicrous speed, just so I can see bull-man in the stream. Fucker is fast, but I'm a little quicker.

Bouncing off walls and furniture, I anticipate bull-man's location.

I get there a fraction before he does, but it is long enough to ram Cal through his stomach.

I feel the sickening give away of flesh, muscles, and organs before the sickening reverberation of Cal hitting something hard, a sting going up my arm. I let go of Cal and slip out of the stream.

The coppery smell of blood hits me like a wall. The scent is everywhere. Bull-man is bellowing in agony, trying to pull a bright red, glowing Cal out. I'm starting to feel dizzy.

Looking down, I realize that I'm covered in blood. I don't remember bull-man profusely bleeding on me when I stabbed him. It is then that I look at bull-man's hands and in one of them is a dagger.

And then I feel it, intense pain on my left side. I rub down my side, trying to find the point of entry. If I can stem the flow enough, so I don't bleed out before the guys get here, I may have a fighting chance.

I found the hole because an agonizing pain tears through my side. Totally unsanitary but totally necessary by sticking my finger in there until I can make some sort of makeshift field dressing. The pain becomes even more intense. So much so that I am falling to my hands and knees. I look around the room to see what I could use to stop the bleeding. Nothing. I take off my tank top and use that to tie around my waist to slow the bleeding. I lay on my right side.

I look to see where bull-man is because it is too fucking quiet. I see him on the floor, Cal still embedded in him, blood flowing out. I start seeing black dots at the edges of my vision.

My head is feeling light, I know I'm in some real fucking trouble. 'Virgil!' crying out in my head. 'HELP!' I'm starting to get sleepy and am having trouble keeping my eyes open. A sense of serenity overtakes me. *Just a quick nap.*

I let me eyes close for a minute…

The searing pain brings me back to awareness. *Let me go back under!* Unfortunately, that prayer IS NOT answered. I crack open my eyes with a groan, my blurry vision sharpening. *Holy shit!*

The gorgeous angel from my dream is looking down at me. He's even more handsome in reality. But the pain is too real for this to be a dream. I take in his red eyes, just staring at me. The eyes that swirl like blood fringed with golden lashes. *Definitely going to nickname him Red.* As in the dream, he has a beautifully sculpted face with a straight aquiline nose, square chin, high cheekbones, and extremely kissable lips.

My perusal of his face lasts ten seconds before I'm clenching my teeth, trying not to scream in agony. Tears and sweat streaming down my face. It's then I notice that the mystery angel has Cal pressed up against the wound on my side, glowing like my energy.

"Cal?" I say softly in my head.

"Yes, little one?" is the response.

"Am I going to die?"

I swear I thought I heard Cal snort. "You are not that lucky. You're very hard to kill and an extremely fast healer. I'm speeding up the healing process. Why you are currently experiencing extreme discomfort." *Discomfort my ass!*

I turn my attention back to Red, focusing hard. "Who are you," I ask? Needing anything to get my mind off the pain.

Red pauses for a moment, processing my question. He opens his mouth and says with a raspy voice that sounds like it has not been used in a long time, "Uriel."

"I'm Sera," I respond. "I'm here to save you."

"Save me? Why?" he asks.

"I was sent by the Creator to free you," I respond.

He nods his head in understanding, keeping Cal on my wound.

We don't speak again for the rest of the time I'm awake. I pass in and out of consciousness when the pain becomes intolerable.

It must have been hours when the pain finally lessens to a dull ache. I wake up, feeling physically exhausted from the rapid healing. I was placed on a soft canopied bed during my recovery. I look around for bull-man, now officially named Red.

Red was not in my immediate vicinity. I slowly sit up and tenderly feel the skin on the side that was stabbed. Not even a scar! Looking around, I now realize where Red initially took us. The room in my dream. I'm laying on red satin sheets bordered with gold, and gaudy golden statues and gold filigree work in every location that I am recalling from my dream. There was one difference to the room though. An open doorway, probably to the bathroom.

Out comes Red with a towel on, wrapped around his hips, water still dripping down his beautiful golden body. And those beautiful red wings! They look so soft that I would love to lie on them.

His golden blond hair is cut military-style. If G looks like a warrior from medieval times, Red looks like a Spartan. Tall and lean, well-defined muscles. Not massive like G or a runner like Virgil but a combination of both. And I feel an immediate attraction to him.

Red sees that I'm awake and gives me a cursory look before walking back into the bathroom. He comes back out with pants and a shirt on. No wings. And he's standing near the doorway staring at a spot below me. I suddenly feel extremely self-aware.

I look down at myself, and I see that I'm head to toe covered in blood. Not too sure if it's all mine or some of Red's blood mixed with mine. I look back at Red, still standing and refusing to look at me. From his posture and the way he's not meeting my eyes, he might be shy and insecure or has no interest in me as the person who freed him.

"Uriel?" I say quietly "I came with two companions, one of them is Gabriel." Red snaps his head up in surprise when I say G's archangel name. "Could you find them in the labyrinth and bring them here? I'm sure they are concerned about my welfare."

Red only nods his head and walks out the only other doorway to leave. *An angel of a few words?*

Taking advantage of Red's exit, I walk into the bathroom. Red tile, gold used for all the bathroom fixtures and gold leaf crown molding around the upper walls.

The walk-in shower was heaven sent. Rain shower head with body jets. Oh, and it's digital. I set the water temperature to really hot and step into the cascade of water with my clothes still on. I don't have anything else to wear at the moment so might as well get those as clean as possible when I can.

When the water running off me becomes clear, I begin undressing.

"SERA!!" My name is bouncing off the walls, an echo created by the tiles.

Taking my boots and socks off while taking a shower was not a smart move. My boots are water-logged and hard to loosen enough for me to pull them off while standing.

Sitting on the tile floor, with the water bouncing off my head, yanking off the last boot and sock was not something I want G or Virgil to see. It makes me look vulnerable.

The bellow sounded really close and really panicked. I am in the process of standing up in the shower barefoot, about to take off my sports bra and untie the shirt around my waist, when I hear voices and boots running into the bathroom. This causes me some alarm because I am now worried that another monster is chasing them. I turn around to face the shower doorway, watching G and Virgil blast through and not stopping until they both have me in their arms.

My heart skips a beat when I see their frantic faces. I was afraid I was never going to see them again when bull-man, aka Red, stabbed me. Now I can see that Virgil and G both had the same fear of losing me.

G picks me up and kisses me hard, reluctant to give me to Virgil.

Virgil gets a hold of me and kisses me the same way, all the fear and relief pouring into the kiss. Somewhere in the background, I hear a throat clearing. I stop kissing Virgil and turn to the source of the noise.

Red is standing at the shower doorway, still refusing to look at me, but looking at G with an admonishing expression. What the hell?! Is he judging us? I untangle myself from Virgil's arms and march straight up to Red. This bullshit ends now!

"What the fuck is your problem, Uriel?" I yell in his face. "You're standing here judging us, but I turned you back from a half-bull, half-man creature because you became the embodiment of Lust. I almost died trying saving you!"

I hear a sharp hiss from behind me.

Didn't want to break my near-death experience to the guys so soon. Or ever. "The least you could do," I keep ranting, "is give me the fucking courtesy to acknowledge my presence!" I turn back to the guys, who are now drenched, but I still need to finish my shower.

I rip my sports bra off, my breasts flying out, and untie the shirt around my waist. Walking back under the scalding water, I take off my pants and panties, turning back to Red, just to see the expression on his face. *Nailed it!* Went for shock value and there is definitely a shocked expression on Red's face. And Red starts turning, well, red. I can't tell if the exasperated look is from being a prude or he's turned on.

I smirk and switch my attention back to the guys. They are in the process of undressing as well. I need my guys like I need air. I turn back to the doorway and Red is gone.

What may have been at least two hours in that shower, because the sex was long, slow, and sweet, all three of us step out of the bathroom, wrapped in plush, white bathroom robes. Being hungry and exhausted, I start looking for my pack.

It is then I notice that Red is on the bed, eating a steak. "Where did you get the steak?" I ask him bluntly, too hungry to beat around the bush.

"I thought it. It came," is Red's response.

"'If you build it, they will come,'" I say, quoting *Field of Dreams* out loud. Red looks at me like I'm a psycho and my guys give me weird looks. Definitely not movie nerds. *Need to fix that.*

Closing my eyes and thinking hard, I visualize a big-ass, 70-inch flat-screen TV on the wall in front of me; made of gold of course. Need to keep within the theme decor. Oh, and unlimited access to all the movies ever made. I also think of a couple of large New York- style brick-oven pizzas. I'm having a movie night. I've earned a little treat and a break.

The smell of fresh, warm pizza hits me before I open my eyes. I see five boxes of neatly stacked pizzas on the bed. I think of a domestic beer in a cool glass, at the right temperature. *Awesome! Who says Hell has to suck all the time?*

I think of a universal remote for the TV, and it appears next to the pizzas. And a big-ass role of paper towels. I grab the remote to turn on the huge TV.

I walk to the bed, grab a pizza box and tear off a couple of towel sheets, then I sit down on the bed, sliding myself and the pizza box to the center while juggling my beer. Good thing I got some practice when I had girl's night at one of my friend's houses.

Then I remember that Beatrice, Mary, and Rachael were never truly my friends. Just divine bodyguards. I start feeling down about that little revelation. *Don't think about it.*

Blocking the sadness, I settle in, opening the pizza box and grabbing a slice. Turning on the TV, I scroll for the newest blockbusters about to be released in theaters. That's when I feel multiple sets of eyes on me. Inward eye roll. *Here it comes.*

Taking a deep breath, I focus my attention on the men in the room. Virgil and G still standing where I left them; G looking like he needs to say something. "What's up?" I ask the room.

G clears his throat, looking extremely uncomfortable. "We can't leave this circle until you save Uriel," he tells me.

"What are you talking about G? I did save him. Look!" I say, pointing at Red, "He's not bull-man anymore!" I say with a little exasperation in my voice.

"He has to help you get stronger for us to get to the next level," Virgil says quietly.

"If you two haven't noticed, Red has no interest in me whatsoever. Won't force him to do anything he doesn't want to do," I say with finality. Red has his back towards me during the entire conversation.

"We are staying in a room Uriel showed us on our way to see you. We are heading over there now." G stares down at the floor. I start sliding to the edge of the bed to go with the guys.

"No, Sera," Virgil says, shaking his head. "You're staying here. With Uriel."

Huffing impatiently, I say, "How long do you both want to stay in this circle? Because I bet that Red is the Archangel of Chastity. And I didn't get his chastity belt key before getting here. So, what do you both suggest I do? We might be here for a very long time." I think I struck a nerve with Red because I see his back stiffening.

G gives me a big grin and a wink. "You never backed away from a challenge before. Don't start now."

Then a thought hits me. "Why don't you ask Red what he wants to do?" I say with a smirk on my face. From the way Red avoids me, he apparently wants me to be with the guys and not stay with him.

"She stays," Red says.

What? I give Red's back a confused stare.

"Then it's settled," G says. Virgil and G walk out of the room, and I'm alone with Red. *Great.*

Because I'm in an uncomfortable situation right now, I chug my beer. The cold and sharp taste hitting the back of my throat. The coldness turns into warmth as the alcohol starts traveling through my body.

I slide to the edge of the bed, getting up to stand in front of Red and try to talk with him. "You want one?" I politely ask, indicating my now empty beer glass.

"No," is his abrupt response.

Studying Red, still sitting at the edge of the bed, I see that his body posture is extremely ridged. "Red," I say, "if I may call you that? I'm going to get you a beer. It will help relax you and maybe get rid of the stick up your ass."

I think of another cup filled with a Belgium blonde import. He looks like the type who might like the taste of an import beer. I try handing the cup to him, but he refuses to take it.

"Red," I say through gritted teeth, my patience short because I am starting to get tired . "Please take the fucking cup, or I'm leaving. You can wallow in your misery alone."

He actually looks up at me, and I see some confusion on his face. But he takes the cup and downs it in one gulp. My mouth pops open in amazement. I quickly close it shut. *Damn!*

I think of a refill for him, and he takes the cup and starts drinking it casually. "Why did you want me to stay?" I ask point blank.

He removes the cup from his beautiful lips and stares straight ahead, avoiding looking at me.

Shrugging his shoulders, he says, "I don't know."

Fine. Too exhausted to attempt more small talk, I walk back to the head of the bed, beer in hand, and slide under the covers. Propping up the pillows behind me to support my sitting position. I put on a romantic comedy because I'm literally stuck in this room with Chastity and I need a good laugh.

Throughout the whole movie, I'm eating, drinking, and laughing. I even hear Red snort and his back shaking at some of the ridiculously hilarious scenes. At least he has a sense of humor.

At the ending credits, I turn off the TV, thinking away the leftovers and garbage, and get up to go into the bathroom. After refreshing myself, and thinking up underwear and comfortable pajamas, I walk out and slide back into the bed.

Red hasn't moved a muscle from the edge of the bed. I think the lights off. "Good night," I say to the pitch-black room. No response. *Jerk.*

Have you ever been so exhausted that you don't dream and wake up with a jolt because you forgot where you are? That's how I feel at the moment. Snapping my eyes open, I have no fucking clue where I am, and I'm panicking.

Memories start flooding in, reminding me I'm in a room, alone with an archangel who doesn't want me, but we can't leave until he does. *Life sucks!*

Calming down, I realize that I'm not alone in the massive bed. Someone is laying close to me. From the muted energy signature, I know it's Red. His energy feels like the worst part of a blizzard, freezing cold and indifferent to anything and everything it comes in contact with. *Must be lonely.*

Then I feel his hand skimming up and down my arm. Red must sense me being awake because I feel his warm breath on my face, inching closer to find my lips in the dark.

I reach my hand out to stop him so I can ask what the fuck is going on, but when I touch his strong shoulder, he grabs my hand and starts sucking on my fingers. Oh! All reservations fly out the window as I am getting wet.

His tongue is amazing! I hope he kisses me soon so I can feel that pleasure in my mouth. As if on cue, he releases the last finger he is sucking on and somehow finds my lips in the pitch-black room.

He kisses me shyly, testing to see if I'll accept his kiss. Realizing that I'm kissing him in return, that encourages him to part my lips and teeth with that articulate tongue, and he delves into my mouth.

Zing! A bolt of energy goes through me. I respond in kind, and I want nothing more but for him to please me and I want to please him. I wrap my arms around his body, wanting him closer to me, to feel his body on top of mine. But he seems hesitant. Slow and gentle.

I scoot closer to him, not breaking our passionate kiss. I lightly run my fingers up and down his bare back, noting that he took his shirt off sometime during the night. His body starts to relax, drawing closer to me. I keep running my fingers up and down his torso, adding a little more pressure so he can get used to my touch.

Getting bolder, I slide my hand down to his bare ass and back up. *Another male model who likes to sleep in the nude.* I keep the movement going, and his kissing is turning frenzied.

He suddenly swoops me into his arms and rolls me on top of him. I'm straddling his stomach, but I get an idea, I've latched onto his earlobe, sucking and nibbling. I suck, nibble, and lick my way down his body. Stopping at his pecks to nip. He groaned when I did that.

I keep venturing down, kissing his belly button and a little past until his large cock presses into my chin. But that doesn't deter me from trying something new.

I delicately put my hand on his shaft, not able to get my fingers around him, and guide the head into my mouth. I hear Red hiss and moan. Using that as a signal to keep going, I start working his cock with my hands and mouth.

Sucking the bulbous head, making him pre-cum. The saltiness and texture are surprisingly good.

Licking and sucking, getting his dick nice and moist, pumping and squeezing the shaft vigorously while his moans are becoming increasingly louder. "Oh fuck!" Red shouts, cum starting to shoot down my throat. "Circe!"

My heart stops, and I go still. An emotional and physical feeling, like getting slapped in the face hits me hard, and a feeling of hurt is burning in my chest. I pull his cock out of my mouth, roll to the side edge of the bed, stand up, think the bathroom lights on, and walk straight in.

Heading straight to the counter, I think myself toothpaste,

toothbrush, and powerful mouthwash. I spend ten minutes sanitizing my mouth, ignoring the emotional hurt.

Finishing, I take a deep breath and march out of the bathroom. Red must have thought the lights on. *Time for some answers.*

He's sitting, hunched over at the edge of the bed with his hands covering his face and fully dressed. I stop walking, standing in front of Red.

"Do you mind telling me what the fuck that was about? Why did you call out another person's name while I was making you cum?" I'm in no mood for tact.

He looks up at me, and I think for the first time since we've met, he actually "sees" me. I stand there, crossing my arms, waiting for his explanation.

I kind of feel sorry for him because his expression is filled with remorse. "I'm sorry," Red gruffly states. I arch an eyebrow, showing that I'm still waiting for an explanation. He sighs. "It was during the war," he begins telling me. "The human casualties caused by the war were devastating. After one particularly bad battle on one of the islands in the Mediterranean, the fallout was the island exploding in half, and I hear crying. I fly towards the sound, realizing that there was a human civilization on the island, now all but gone. I fly past the destroyed ancient city, most of it fell into the ocean, flying towards a remote part of the island where the land turns into a rocky, mountainous landscape. I was able to trace the sound to a cave in one of the hills. There was a cave-in caused by the battle, and I dug the only survivor out. Circe."

Red stops and sighs again, a small, sad smile appearing on his lips. "As an Archangel, I'm the embodiment of the heavenly virtue Chastity, so I've never experienced any sort of physical attraction to any being. When I first laid eyes on her, I felt like I was struck by lightning and I wanted her. I could tell that she was attracted to me too. We became lovers, and my obsession for her got stronger. Strong enough that I became derelict in my sacred duty. Which was protecting humans and preventing them to revert to their base animal urges through sex."

He stops again and closes his eyes, a painful grimace appearing. "She asked me to fly her to the outskirts of another civilization. She said that she was a healer and wanted to feel useful again. I would have done anything to make her happy. So, I did what she asked. Even built a place for us to live. She would go out every day, visiting and healing people in the community, but she would return before the sunset. Then the visits would turn into overnight stays; she explained that people in the city had heard of her talents and needed her. I asked her if she needed my help with anything or just to accompany her into the city. She refused my help. It was then that I noticed how cold and distant she'd become and that we had stopped making love. I became suspicious of her and one day decided to follow her. I found out that she became a temple priestess and 'served' the entire city. There was nothing that could satisfy her lust. That knowledge destroyed me, making me want to ruin anything good that I had left in me. So, I screwed everyone, making false promises to be faithful. I was rutting like a beast, until one day, I physically became a beast. Lucifer found and collected me, sending me here to this circle. To protect the door going to the next circle."

"Was Circe the same sorceress Circe from the Greek mythology?" I ask.

"Yes. And, you look exactly like her, except you have short hair," he adds.

Okay? "Wait a minute," I say, needing to clarify something. "Are you the Minotaur in the Greek mythology story?"

Red just shrugs his shoulders to acknowledge my correct assessment.

"I can't help my physical appearance," I tell him, "but I'm not nor would I ever be like her." Then I get an idea. "Which element does your power have an affinity for?" He looks up at me in shock.

"How do you know about an Archangel's affinity power?" he questions me like a detective.

Looking him straight in the eye without blinking, I say, "G trained me in his affinity power element of air. Maybe you can help train me in yours?" I suggest. "Or maybe some self-defense? I was only trained in sword fighting by G. Maybe you can show me different moves or maybe techniques?"

He doesn't respond.

"I'm sorry that bitch did that to you," I tell him truthfully. "But not all women are like that. Anyway, I'm going back to sleep. Have a good night." Red just nods his head. I'm feeling deflated.

I think of a new bedroom attached to this one with an open doorway. Complete with the most comfortable queen size bed ever made. Grabbing Cal, I walk into my new bedroom and slip under the covers of my satin sheets. I close my eyes, nodding off.

CHAPTER 12

And More Fucking Training

Something is shaking me. *Or someone.* My eyes open, and Red is shaking my shoulders.

"What, Red?" I ask.

"Time to train," he says.

Great! Because I had such an awesome night!

"Give me a second to get ready," I tell him. Red walks out, and I think of a workout outfit, complete with sneakers. I sling Cal on and walk out of my bedroom. And immediately come to a halt.

The main room is no longer a bedroom but a gymnasium. A big gymnasium with floor and wall mats. My training with G in Limbo and on the boat comes to mind.

Immediately I feel out to locate Red and sense him right behind me. I spin around and simultaneously slip into the stream. It doesn't help me to avoid the fist swung into my stomach. Fuck! Dropping to my knees and holding my stomach, I'm doing anything I can to avoid puking. My eyes are blurring from unshed tears. I see Red's boots stop right in front of me. "G didn't teach you shit about hand to hand combat."

All I could do is roll my eyes at the mat floor and try not to pass out.

When the puking sensation passes, I gingerly stand up to my feet. Looking at Red, I'm watching him assess me.

"You have no stamina, strength, and coordination. I'm surprised you've lived this long."

I just stare at him, showing that his criticism does not affect me.

"You need to run, swim and lift weights. Swimming will help with the stamina and quickly build your muscles. First things first, we need to get your ass into a pool."

I think up an Olympic size swimming pool about five-feet deep with lane lines, a one-piece swimsuit, swim cap, and goggles. Red flushes, seeing me in a swimsuit. I perform a shallow dive in. I think the water temperature up to where I cannot get hypothermia.

From what I can remember from my swim team years, I start my freestyle stroke, going down the pool and back twice as a warm-up. I'm already breathing heavy. *Shit I have no stamina!*

I stop at Red's boots near the pool edge and stand, placing my goggles above my eyes. I'm waiting for Red to give me guidance on how I can quickly increase my stamina. He drops a rope with two loops and a tail he's still holding onto next to me.

"Place your feet through the loops, up to your ankles. Here." Red hands me two rocks, each weighing at least ten pounds. I place the stones at the edge to get my feet through the rope loops. I put my goggles back over my eyes.

Picking up the rocks I wait for Red. He pulls the rope, tightening the loops around my ankles where I cannot kick, and sweeping my legs from underneath me. I let my body float and just use my arms with the weights to start my strokes.

I think I last about ten minutes until I could not lift my arms. I hear Red say, "Stop," releasing the rope. "Switch the loops to your wrists." I comply. "Float on your back, use the wall to push out with your hands and when you feel the rope tighten, dolphin kick." I do as he says. I last a lot longer.

"Stop," I hear. I put my legs down. "Get out." Jumping out of the pool, I think myself dry.

Nice!

The pool completely disappears, and a dirt circular track appears in its place. I think of running gear to wear.

"When I tell you to jog, you jog. When I say sprint, you sprint," Red commands. I nod my head in understanding. "Jog," Red says.

Between the jogging and running, I make it eight times around the track before I start heaving. I sit immediately and think of a full water bottle. I carefully sip the cold water between catching my breath and not choking.

While I'm recovering, I feel G's and Virgil's presences in the room.

"Get up." Red's commanding voice is exceptionally close to me. Using my hands to help boost me onto my wobbly legs, I'm still hunching over, trying to slow my heart rate. I gently lift my torso and look into swirling blood-red eyes. Those eyes carry the look of anger and disappointment.

"We are going to practice some sparring and basic self-defense moves," Red says no more than three feet away from me. He walks past me, and I turn to follow him, noting that the dirt track is now a big sparring mat. I have a feeling my ass is going to get handed to me.

I hate being right. Red shows me a lot of throwing techniques, mostly me getting thrown to the mat. He also teaches me how to properly punch and make me hit his hands over and over again in a sequence of jabs, crosses, and uppercuts.

Beating his hands is like hitting iron. I have a hard time of getting my fingers to open after what feels like fifteen minutes. We must have been on the mat for about an hour. "Stop," Red commands. I'm so sore that the only thing that doesn't hurt is my hair.

"You will eat, shower, and relax for a few hours. Then you will do some sword sparring with G." Red turns his head to stare at G, still standing on the side with Virgil. There must have been some kind of silent exchange because G lowers his head like he just has had his ass chewed out. He silently nods his head.

"After sparring with G, you will work with Virgil on teaching you force fields and making people lose immediate consciousness." I turn towards Virgil, looking at him with shock. I feel like an ass for underestimating him. Virgil just gives me an embarrassed smile and shrugs his shoulders. Red continues, "This will be your workout schedule every day until I feel that you are ready to survive the next circle."

"What is the next circle?" I ask.

"Gluttony," is Red's response.

CHAPTER 13

SURVIVING GLUTTONY

Training with the guys every day for the first few days was excruciatingly painful, but I was starting to become stronger, faster, and a better fighter.

It has felt like weeks that have passed by because Hell has no clock, I am feeling solid and sure in my fighting abilities. Red still hands me my ass when we are practicing hand to hand combat; but I wasn't getting thrown as often, learning how to dodge his throwing moves.

G taught me many different sword fighting styles and techniques, like how to disarm another opponent or swiftly and cleanly take off someone's head or an appendage.

Virgil shows me how to throw up force fields and how to knock people out with one touch. Having arrows and knives bouncing off around you could get frightening, especially when you're extremely exhausted from the grueling training in the morning and the hour of a sword sparring session with G.

And zapping people to sleep is much harder than it looked when Virgil zapped me to sleep when we first met at the bar. The best I can do is zap Virgil's arm to sleep. And that's when I'm really trying! Otherwise, he tells me to stop tickling him.

However, Red still will not tell what element his power has an affinity to and will not let me train on elemental energy. Red still does not trust me.

This morning is starting no difference except I can swim for a hell of a lot longer and run a hell of a lot farther. Red and I go to spar on the mat, and I face him, preparing for his attack. Instead of thinking about how he's going to attack me, I drift into myself, feeling at peace; and like with G when we are sword fighting, I am able to anticipate his move.

I slip into the stream faster than ever, dodging Red, grabbing his outstretched arm and pulling his body into mine while I'm twisting and using my shoulder and hip as leverage to throw him to the mat. But I don't stop, instinct kicks in and I'm going with the flow, no longer overthinking things.

I follow Red down to the mat, able to tap into my energy for strength to pin him down and get him into a side arm-bar. Red is able to get out of the arm-bar and quickly uses a move I've never seen to put me on my back.

I land with a thud, with Red in between my legs, pinning my hands down to the mat. I try to move my arms, but his hands are like cement foundations, not moving at all. I try moving my lower body, but Red weighs a freaking ton! And then I feel his arousal. Uh?

I stop my thrashing, turning my head to look into his eyes. They are swirling, and I see want in them. I raise my hips to rub myself against him while wrapping my legs around his waist, locking my ankles behind his back.

He lowers his body onto mine, lowering his head. I meet him midway, and we start kissing each other with need. He starts rubbing himself between my legs, his giant cock hitting my clit perfectly.

I've been training so much that I've been too tired for sex. My body is now letting me know it's been a while and it needs a release. But he's still unaware of what would happen when we do have sex.

I gently break our kiss. Red starts kissing my neck. "Red—"

"Mmmmhmmm," is his reply into my neck.

"Red, I want you to trust me. So, I'm letting you know that if we have sex, you and I will be mated. And you will also be one of my eight mates, along with G and Virgil, forever."

Red stops then raises his head to look down at me with a look of pure astonishment and anger on his face. I feel him going cold and starting to stand up. I unwrap my legs, and Red gets up, not bothering to look at me. Red walks away, leaving me on the mat, in the gym, alone.

For once I want to fly away. *Might as well try something different.*

I remember the times my wings have come out. I always felt euphoric and at peace. All I could do now is forgive Red for rejecting me, washing away the pain; making me feel that peace and in that peace comes euphoria.

Centering myself and finding the peace I need, I turn my head, seeing that my fiery wings have come out. I keep that peaceful feeling, and I jump into the air. And I come back down to the ground. My wings are still there.

I think of my wings as appendages connected to me. Like an arm or a leg, I think of moving just one wing. I'm able to spread the wing all the way out. It's like stretching a muscle. I do the same on the other wing. I flap both wings, feeling the strain of muscles never used in my back. Need to start building those muscles.

I keep my wings fully extended, and I jump. I perform two flaps to get a little higher, holding the wings spread to float down. I respect G even more for when for hours we descended slowly down lust hill. I do this two more times, until the muscles in my back are fatigued and I am shaking.

I let go of that peaceful feeling, my wings disappearing. Sweaty and tired, I walk into my room and into my own bathroom designed to look like a spa. Walking over to the jacuzzi tub, I turn on the hot water, anticipating the physical relief I will feel.

Soaking in the jacuzzi tub for an hour, I let the water out, wrapping myself in a plush, white bathrobe. I walk over to the bed to sit, thinking of a cheese omelet with fresh fruit on the side. Need to eat healthier to stay light.

I quickly finish eating, and the pain of Red's rejection hits me like a freight train. I start tearing up, and I lay down on the bed, thinking away my dirty plate and utensils. The tears start streaming down my face and a sob escapes my lips. I don't know how long I cry until I pass out.

Gently being shaken, I open my eyes. My eyes feel swollen and gritty like I've been crying my heart out. *Oh wait, I have.* I look up and see Virgil and G. They both have concerned looks on their faces.

"Where's Red?" G asks.

"I don't know," I respond.

"What happened?" Virgil asks.

"I told him about being mated for life if we have sex," I bluntly state.

"And…?" G demands.

"And he left." This is all I would allow the guys to know. G and Virgil look at each other, nodding their heads in some unspoken agreement, and both walk out of my bedroom. *What?*

Fresh tears stream down my face, but I'm too tired to wipe them away. I close my eyes and go back to sleep.

CHAPTER 14

BULL-HEADEDNESS...

"WHAT THE FUCK!"

I wake to sounds of fighting and a lot of shouting. I sit up in my soft bed, thinking the lights on, and I hear the sounds of struggling in the next room, coming my way. A second later, the source of the commotion bursts into my bedroom.

I am shocked into silence at the scene before me. G comes in first with a roughed-up Red in a choke hold while Virgil is carrying Red's legs. Virgil drops Red's legs, allowing G to get Red into a proper choke hold so he can force his head up.

"Look at her!" G hisses into Red's ear. Red turns his eyes to me, his face softening. "She's hurt because of you! There are a lot of things I can endure, but Sera crying is not one of them. Fix it. Now!" G growls with more than a hint of a threat in his voice.

G lets go of his choke hold on Red and walks out the door with Virgil. Leaving me alone with Red. I'm too exhausted to have it out with Red and I want to return to the comforting blackness of sleep. I think the lights off and roll back over to give my mind back to slumber. *I don't want to deal with this right now.*

Waking up, I'm ready for a new training day. Looking around, I see that Red has left the room during the night. Not caring at this point but just wanting to get through another rough day, I think on my training outfit (yoga pants, tank top, sports bra, and running shoes) and walk towards the doorway. Going to practice flying if Red is not here. Walking out, I see the place where we train has turned back into a bedroom. The bed is empty and no sign of Red. *Figures he will run from this problem.*

I think of the gymnasium space, instantly transforming the room. I find that peaceful, euphoric feeling again, releasing my fiery wings. Just like the day before, I jump into the air, flap twice to get some height, and then float to the ground.

I'm in mid-flap on my sixth set when I feel Red's energy presence behind me. I climb a little higher than before, floating down to the ground. When I land softly on my feet, I turn around.

Red's face has an expression of awe on it. "What?" I ask him.

"You never mentioned you have wings," Red says quietly.

"You never asked," I prissily reply.

"I'm sorry I hurt you.".

I casually shrug my shoulders. "Don't worry, I got over it," I say, pretending that nothing major has happened between us.

Red's facial expression, however, changes from looking contrite to pissed off.

What did I do? "I'm sorry, but is there something I missed?" I ask him. I lose that peaceful feeling, my wings disappearing. "Why are you angry at me? I told you the truth so you can see that I'm trustworthy. You could have at least made your decision about it with a little more grace," I tell him hotly.

Red starts stalking towards me. I hold my ground. I'm not going to let him try to cower me.

Red gets to an inch away from my face. "You're acting like it is not bothering you, is bothering me."

Shaking my head, I snort, "That's the most fucked up reasoning for someone like you to get 'bothered.'"

"Someone like me?" he asks angrily.

"Yeah, someone like you! Someone who's cold and indifferent to other people's feelings. You got hurt by your ex. So fucking what? That's a common occurrence. Eventually, you have to move on. Taking your hurt and anger out on me, the only other person, I'm guessing, you ever had an attraction to since, makes me not want to know you!" I shout angrily at him. "Now, if you don't want me, please fuck off and leave me be!" I'm still standing my ground, my body shaking in the hot fury that has taken over my reasoning. I definitely struck a nerve because he looks as pissed as I feel. *Good!*

Red takes a deep breath and steps away from me. And then turns to leave! *Coward!* I tap into my energy, creating a fireball, and launch it at Red. The fireball's impact has enough force for Red to fly face first into the ground. I'm so fucking pissed that angry tears are streaming down my face. Red turns his head and, without me even realizing it, slips into the stream, and I'm lying on the mat with him on top of me, between my legs, holding my arms down. *De ja vu.*

This time he brutally assaults my mouth, not letting go of my arms. Red takes my arms, slides them above my head, and pins my wrists down with one hand. He takes his free hand and tears my yoga pants and panties off me like they were made out of wrapping paper and my pussy is a hotly desired gift. He finds my clit, rubbing and circling it with his thumb. I'm dripping wet and thrusting my hips up, showing how much I want him.

Red undoes his pants buttons and pulls out his massive cock, guiding it to my damp entrance. Without ceremony, he thrusts into me. He's big! Almost too big.

I groan into his mouth, precariously balanced between sweet pleasure and pain. He doesn't break our kiss as he starts thrusting deeper and deeper into me until he's all the way to the hilt. And then he starts pounding into me, not letting my wrists go, his mouth still devouring mine. He doesn't slow but keeps on going, my clit being perfectly rubbed until an enormous orgasm rips through my body, making me release a scream into Red's mouth.

Red stops kissing, looking down at me with utter confusion while I'm riding wave after wave of pleasure, the muscles in my pussy squeezing his huge cock. He stops thrusting into me. "Am I hurting you?" he asks, a look of deep concern on his face.

Smiling brightly, I say "No. You gave me an orgasm." My statement must have confused him more. "Didn't you ever give your ex an orgasm?" I inquire.

"She always screamed, but I never felt her milk me. Ever," Red answers demurely.

I had to suppress a knowing grin. "I'm sorry, Red, but she was faking it. If you keep going, you could get a few more out of me," I politely tell him, while hoping beyond hope he'll not stop.

I don't need to tell him twice. He starts pounding into me again, thrusting nice and deep. I feel the pleasure building up again. "Right there! Keep going!" I yell. He complies and thrusts into me harder and faster. "OH FUCK!" and I come hard. So hard that I feel my soul leave my body and is surrounded in warm, white light. I'm peaceful and happy. And then I came back down to earth again.

When my eyes refocus, Red has a shocked expression on his face. I look to the left, seeing my wings have popped out. I give him a small smile. "That's my body enjoying your lovemaking."

He grins, still thrusting into me, but slower and gentler. Red starts to pick up the pace again, and before I know it, another orgasm overwhelms me with Red coming also. A look of both agony and ecstasy is on his face, his neck straining, "Fuck, Sera!" he yells to the sky. His crimson wings pop out while he's shooting his cum deep within me.

He definitely enjoyed that!

A few more thrusts and he collapses on top of me. He releases my wrists, using both hands to hold my face while gently kissing me. "That was very nice," I tell him. Red chuckles and moves his head up to where he can look down at me. For the first time, I see happiness in his eyes. I hope he never regrets becoming one of my eight mates.

Scooping me up, Red turns over onto his back and tucks one of his beautiful wings under me. I never realized how good Red smells until now. Being this close to his body, Red's personal musk reminds me of freshly baked gingerbread cookies, and the nostalgia of home and comfort hits me. He wraps his arm around me, snuggling me close, his finger lightly rubbing up and down my arm. Feeling safe, I'm starting to feel drowsy and close my eyes.

It's black, entirely black. I hear a woman screaming from somewhere in the dark. I start moving in the direction of the screaming. As I'm getting closer, the blackness begins to fade, getting lighter and lighter until I'm watching what could be a scene from the TV show ER.

Nurses scrambling all over, their hospital gowns and scrubs covered in blood. The doctor is in front of a woman who is in the process of giving birth. The woman is a beautiful brunette or would be considered attractive if she were not covered in sweat and screaming in agony. A handsome blond man is standing next to her, holding her hand, concern, and fear on his face.

"Push!" the doctor says and starts counting to ten. At ten, the doctor says, "Okay, relax. Breathe." The woman relaxes, giving the man a teary-eyed smile. "Okay, Diana," the doctor states, "push!" and the doctor starts counting again. "The head is out!" the doctor says excitedly, "keep pushing!".

I'm guessing the rest of the baby comes out. "It's a girl!" the doctor says joyously. The doctor hands the baby to a nurse.

I look towards the delivery table to see how the woman is fairing. Her skin is pale, almost a gray color. The heart monitor she is connected to suddenly sounds an alarm. I'm not paying attention to what the doctor is saying because the woman is staring right at me! She turns her head to look at the man by her side. "Promise me to call her Seraphim," she says pleadingly, as if she knows that the alarms are telling her that her time is short.

"I promise," the man states, his face remains stoic while his eyes are trying not to give away of how truly scared he is.

"I love you," she whispers to him and then closes her eyes.

"We are losing her!" the doctor yells.

I snap my eyes open, sit up, and place my head between legs to prevent me from hyperventilating. "Sera, what's wrong?" Red asks, sitting up with me, rubbing my back, trying to comfort me.

"I just had a dream or maybe a vision? I think I witnessed my mother giving birth to me and dying right after," I say with a sob. Red just keeps rubbing my back. "What does this mean?" I ask him, not trying to hide the fear in my voice.

"Your powers are manifesting to where you can start seeing past events," Red responds.

Letting out a frustrated groan, "That's was a really shitty way of letting me know I can see into the past," I say grumpily.

"When you get stronger, you will be able to see into the future as well," Red calmly states.

Really? I turn to him, "How do you know that?".

Red shrugs. "My magic's affinity is for Spirit. I can see into the past, which is easy. But the future is always flowing in different directions."

I grin at him. "'Always changing, the future is,'" I say, quoting Yoda from *Star Wars.*

"Exactly," Red replies, probably not knowing that I quoted a movie. I sigh. "Now what do we do?"

He gives me a mischievous grin. "We now train harder."

Had to ask.

Later on, Virgil and G arrive to train me on their specialty skills. From the looks of relief on their faces, I'm guessing that they somehow know Red is now part of the "family."

Because I missed a day of training with Virgil and G, they made sure I make up for the lost time by kicking the shit out of me longer than usual. In my training session with Virgil, I create a stronger and bigger shield. Virgil is testing my strength by creating and throwing every projectile ever designed (except a nuclear missile) at it, seeing how long I can keep up the shield.

"Come on, Sera! Hold that shield up!" Virgil yells at me.

Feeling my energy running on empty, I dig down deep for one last push to keep the shield going. Having the shield last for another ten minutes, my nose starts to run. No need to wipe because I know that it's blood. Just like with G on the boat, I collapse.

Waking up didn't hurt as much as the first time when I tried to break the bond with G. I slowly sit up, seeing that someone has changed my clothes to a comfortable tank top and flannel pants and put me in a sizeable fucking bed. And I have three gorgeous guys surrounding me, all asleep, in the nude. *What did I do to deserve this treat?*

Virgil cracks one of his eyes open and smiles at me, sitting up as well. "Because you're a good girl," he teases.

I knew it! "How long have you been able to read my mind?"

"This is the first time I can actually hear your thoughts. The other times were more like reading emotions, not always clear," he says.

"I'm guessing it's because of my new bond with Red causing my power to grow," I say matter-of-factly.

"Yes, it is," responds Virgil.

"How long have I been out this time?"

"A few hours," replies Virgil.

Yes! A better recovery time.

Virgil looks down, but I feel remorse emanating from him. Does he feel bad about pushing me too hard? "Virgil, it's okay. I need to know how far I can be pushed and what to look for when my physical energy is depleted," I softly tell him. He's still looking down at the bed and feeling contrite, so I sidle up to him and kiss him on the lips. He crushes me into him, and I open my mouth to receive his tongue. I hear Virgil chuckle deep in his throat.

He lays me down on the bed, kissing me deeply with need, his hand going underneath my tank top to fondle my breast, making my nipple pucker. I start getting really wet between my legs. I remove my tank top, looking forward to what's going to happen next.

I then hear Red and G stirring, and I break my kiss with Virgil. G slides over to me and takes my mouth with his. I feel my flannel pants being pulled down. I'm commando. *Obviously, a man dressed me.*

Virgil is softly laughing and then starts kissing my stomach, moving his luscious lips down my hip bone to my inner thigh. He uses his finger to separate my moist folds gently and starts licking my pussy.

Meanwhile, G breaks his kiss with me and takes a nipple into his mouth, sucking and nibbling on it. Red takes over, kissing me deeply and passionately. My senses are going into overdrive, with my pleasure spots being activated all at once. I feel an orgasm coming. Virgil then starts sucking my clit, bringing me over the edge. I scream my pleasure into Red's mouth.

"We are just getting started, baby girl," I hear G say.

Bring it!

"She just challenged us," Virgil tells the guys.

Red stops kissing me, giving me a wicked smile. I look at G and Virgil, also giving me evil smiles. I return their smiles.

Red grabs me by the waist to place me on top of him. I decide to try something different. "Scoot back to the headboard and sit up," I tell Red. Still holding me, he shifts us back until he's resting against the headboard. I turn my body around, sitting reverse, facing G and Virgil. I place my fingers into my sopping wet pussy and then take that wetness to rub into my ass.

When I'm friendly and wet in the rear, I take Red's massive cock, and I raise myself on my knees to slowly lower myself onto him. It is slow going, but I eventually work myself all the way onto him, feeling stretched and full. Both G and Virgil are stroking themselves, waiting for me to get comfortable with Red's massive size.

I slowly start riding Red, the fullness beginning to dissipate and turn into pleasure. I then nod at G and Virgil. I lean back against Red's muscular chest, still riding his cock. Red takes a nipple in his hand, squeezing and playing with me with those beautiful hands of his. Virgil comes in between my legs, sliding his massive dick into my pussy. The pleasure is intense.

G slides next us and stands to where my mouth can easily suck his cock. I have no reservations and take hold of the shaft, placing my mouth over the bulbous head and start stroking and sucking. Virgil is thrusting into me hard, and Red grabs my waist by both hands to slam his dick into my ass. I am a bomb ready to explode. I orgasm with such force that I again leave my body, only seeing a bright white light, and feel entirely blissful. The sensation also lasts much longer.

I come back to my body, screaming my release on G's cock while my pussy is milking Virgil. The guys aren't done with me yet. G and Virgil gently pull out of my mouth and pussy, and Red gently raises me up to slide out of my ass. It was like someone said, "Switch!" in their heads.

Red slides down to lay on the bed, turning me around to face him, lowering me down to slide his cock into my pussy. Pulling down enough to where G can get his dick into my ass. Virgil stands near Red's head, and I grab his dick to put into my mouth.

Both G and Red start working me while I'm working Virgil. Another mind-shattering orgasm hits me like a bullet train. I come so hard that the muscles squeezing G's and Red's cocks are strong enough to get them to release in me, surprising them. My screams of pleasure send a strong vibration down Virgil's cock, causing him to orgasm. I hear from all three guys at once, "Fuck, Sera!"

I win! And then I feel it. That physical energy I've only felt once when Virgil and I were at the door in the Limbo. I gently remove Virgil's cock from my mouth, about to ask what's happening, when Red says in awe, "Shit!" I look into his eyes and see him staring at something behind us. I turn my head, and there is a big red door. Hell and its red doors.

"What does it mean?" I ask the guys.

"It means," Red says calmly, "it's time for us to go to the next circle."

Frustration takes over, "Hell sucks!" I whine.

We quickly get up, all of us heading to the bathroom to shower. We take our time cleaning, mostly the guys cleaning me, and I wash them. When we get out of the shower and think ourselves dry, Red informs us that "Hell gets colder and colder with each circle we reach."

I think of practical clothing that is good for wear and tear and will keep me warm if I get too cold. Looking into the mirror, I'm wearing soft, red leather pants that hug and taper down my legs, a red, soft leather halter top, and a spring leather jacket in black. I think of my footwear, seeing that my boots are also black in soft leather, made to hug my legs all the way to an inch below my knees. The boots are flat, and the soles are made to keep traction with the floor.

All three men stare at me, looking like they want to go for another round in the bed. I just smile and walk out of the bathroom. The guys think on their own clothes, mostly tactical clothing with cargo pants, undershirts, long-sleeve shirts, and tactical boots. *They're so hot!* Virgil gives me a knowing grin.

We think of our bags and restock our supplies. Red thinks of his own bag and items to bring. I get Cal and sling the sword across my back.

"You ready, little one"' Cal asks.

"As I'll ever be," I answer.

All four of us approach the door. I look at Virgil. "Let me guess, I'm the only one who can open it?" I ask, motioning to the door.

"Yep," is his reply.

I touch the door and a new saying appears: "If it's yellow, let it mellow. If it's brown, flush it down." *Classy.*

"Lucifer has a really fucked up sense of humor," I say, the annoyance reflecting in my voice. I push the door open, and just like the first door, nothing but darkness.

"G and Virgil, hold on to each other, and I'll hold on to Sera," Red commands.

Red is definitely higher in rank than G in the archangel army.

Red takes my hand and we step through. But there is nothing substantial underneath my feet. I let out a surprised squeal when my stomach hits my throat. Seeing the door getting smaller below me instead of above me makes me realize that either we are falling up, or I'm upside down.

Red flips us upright, then snaps out his wings to control the speed of our descent. Thank goodness I wore my leather coat because it's starting to get a little cold the further down we go. Unlike lust hill, this fall doesn't last half as long, but we don't see the ground until we hit it because of the blackness.

My knees buckle underneath me from the impact, causing me to fall forward on my hands. I get up, and it is only pitch black. I inwardly feel out and see Red's energy signature. I look up to see G and Virgil coming down.

"You're almost to the bottom, G!" I yell up at him. They hit the ground but not as hard as Red and I did.

"Why is there no light?" I ask in the darkness.

"Because I don't feel like letting you four see." *Who said that?!* The voice sounds familiar, as if from a dream, yet crazed.

"Lucifer!" Red yells. "Turn on the lights, or I'm going to shove my holy sword down your throat! You know why we are here! You lost the fucking bet, so man up and stop being a sore loser!"

"Are you sure you want me to do that?" the voice says teasingly with a hint of a threat.

"Guys," I say, grabbing Cal. "I have an awful feeling about what would happen if the lights turn on."

There is a sound of deranged laughter around us that's similar to the Joker's laugh in all those DC Comic movies.

"Cal, what's in the blackness?" I ask in my head.

"There are no energy signatures," Cal says, "meaning that whatever is in the room, its only purpose is to feed and grow."

"Like bacteria?" I ask.

"Yes, little one, but much less complex," answers Cal.

"A one-cell organism," I state matter-of-factly. *Shit!*

"What creature is a one-cell organism, its only purpose is to feed, can only grow in light, and resides in Hell?" I ask the darkness.

I hear clapping, and that maniacal yet now excited voice says "Oh, I know, I know! This question was on Jeopardy last night!"

Such a child!

"Shut the fuck up, Lucifer!" Red yells.

G answers my question with, "Incubi."

"That is correct, Gabriel! And because it was a Daily Double, you get the lights on!" the deranged voice now sounding like Alec Trebek. "Let there be light!" and in a flash, the place is as bright as a Saharan Desert.

My eyes are taking a second to focus when I look around and exclaim, "Holy shit!".

Of course, as fucked up as Hell can get, this circle is even more beautiful than the First Circle. A tropical paradise with pink, sandy beaches and an ocean so blue and turquoise, it could never exist on earth.

And then I see it, in the beautiful pink sand. A blackness is spreading, like cancer but tripling in size every second that goes by.

"Cal," I think, "if the Incubi cannot survive in darkness, is there any way you can create darkness to kill this parasite?"

Cal's answers, "Yes, little one, but I won't be able to kill it, just stop the spreading for a short time."

And then a brilliantly bad idea pops into my head. "Cal, we need something that can suck up light and is extremely powerful. Something like a black hole. I'm going to bluff and call Lucifer out on his bullshit."

"Sounds good to me, little one. May I suggest we make an extremely tiny black hole so you and your mates can get away from the gravitational pull or to close the hole if Lucifer agrees to play nicely?" Cal responds.

Good idea! "Hey, guys, when I say, 'Run!' we need to run that way!" I tell my mates, pointing at the tropical forest.

"Why?" Red demands.

"I don't want to give the game up so please trust me?" I tell him.

Red looks at G and Virgil, both nodding their heads.

Red closes his eyes and takes a deep breath, saying, "Okay," and then reopens his eyes to look straight at me.

I give him a tight smile. "Thank you," I say quietly. *It's a start.*

"Cal. Ready?" I ask in my head.

Cal turns pitch black. "Ready. Just lightly touch the sand," Cal instructs.

I take a deep breath. "Run!" I yell while barely grazing Cal on top of the sand. I slip into the stream, grabbing Virgil as if he weighs nothing, and toss him over my shoulder in a fireman's carry, knowing that Virgil cannot slip into the stream with the rest of us. Red and G are on either side of us. We are hauling ass, but before I know it, we are on a new beach. *We are on an island!*

I've got one more card up my sleeve. "Oh, Lucifer!" I yell sarcastically into the air. "What do you call a mass that has a gravitational pull so strong it collapses on itself?"

A second passes before I get a response. "What Is a black hole?" a bored voice says.

"Ding! Ding! Ding! Guess what I put in the sand on the other side of the island?" I yell back.

"What?" Lucifer's voice still sounding bored. And then as if it is a revelation to, the disembodied voice blurts out, "You didn't?!"

"Yep!" I yell happily, "so if you want your Second Circle to keep existing, I suggest you put your Incubi back in its dark box. Because there is nothing in this universe more gluttonous than a black hole!"

"You cheated!" Lucifer's response sounds like a petulant child.

All I can do is smile. "Is that a yes or no that you will put your little creation away?"

Lucifer, still sounding petulant, says, "Fine, but you need to uncreate a black hole. Good luck with that feat!"

Rolling my eyes, I turn my thoughts back to Cal. "We need to uncreate a black hole. Can we do it?"

"Yes, little one, but it's going to drain you severely."

I just outwitted the Devil. *Let's do this!*

I slip into the stream, going ludicrous speed back to our arrival location. About fifty feet away I feel the gravitational pull, like a vacuum sucking me towards something. I slip out of the stream. I can see something nearly invisible in the place where I grazed Cal in the sand. A rotating distortion, bending the sand and surrounding area about half a foot out that is hovering two feet above the sand about an inch wide.

"Cal, we are here," I inform in my head. Cal turns into the purest white I have ever seen.

"You need to get as close to the black hole as possible and stick me in it."

I drop my pack onto the ground and quickly rummage through the front pockets. Knowing G, he probably packed some rope for emergencies. My hand lands on a spool of five-fifty chord. *Called it!*

Tying the chord around the hilt on Cal, knotting and melting the knot, I lay Cal on the ground, blade towards the growing distortion, slowly giving the chord slack and letting gravity do the work by pulling Cal in. Cal is no less a than a foot away from the center of the somewhat invisible vortex when I see a huge fucking problem.

Cal is starting to become distorted, the blade slowly bending under the unseen gravitational forces. Theoretically, black holes are gravitational anomalies that can bend and break space and time, causing any type of matter to bend and tear apart before ever getting to the center of the hole. However, there is one theory that matter will not be affected if said matter entered dead center, never touching the outer swirling part of the black hole, aka the event horizon.

I feel two energy signatures behind me, knowing that those energies belong to G and Red.

"Sera?" Red says quietly. "What are you doing with that sword?"

Responding, I say, "I need to stab the center of the black hole to close it."

Red is on "detective" mode, asking, "How do you know that?"

I sigh, pointing at the floating sword "Cal told me," I calmly state.

"Cal?" Red asks. I don't bother to look at him. I hear the "she's batshit crazy" tone in his voice.

"Cal, short for Excalibur, talks to her," G tells Red. Nothing but silence. I quickly turn my head to look at Red. He's staring at me with a look of shock and wonder. *Ask him about that later.*

Back to the task at hand, I need to propel Cal as fast as the speed of light, dead center, so it won't get sucked in and destroyed by the event horizon.

I pull Cal back to me. I look at G. "Have you ever propelled anything as fast as the speed of light using your air element?" G is looking at me like I have two heads. "I guess that is a no," I say, turning back to the black hole, now three inches wide in diameter. *How do I get Cal dead center?*

"Little one," Cal says in my head, "the best thing about magic is that magic has no boundaries."

Feeling out to the black hole to detect the energy signatures, I'm amazed at what I'm I seeing: a kaleidoscope of energies, bright at the outer edge, dimming to nearly black at the event horizon. In the center of the black hole is a small spot of pure light, reminding me of my own energy signature. I feel out to that energy signature and, surprisingly, it does feel like my own well of energy.

Calming myself, I feel confident, my wings popping out. Focusing on the energy in the center of the black hole, I turn my own energy into a magnet, slowly drawing out the energy. But it's not enough; the center of the black hole is getting larger instead of smaller. I call for more power, seeing that I'm able to draw out more energy faster. Cal wasn't wrong about my energy going to be severely drained.

The energy in the center of the black hole is getting smaller and smaller over time, but I'm starting to get exhausted. I also know I won't make it to where I'm able to stab the center at the rate I'm drawing the energy. I ask for even more power, sucking out the energy within the black hole like a suction tube. I start feeling the wetness dripping from my nose. *Shit! A little more!*

The energy in the center of the black hole is very dim, the hole itself smaller than a pin drop. "Now, little one!" Cal yells in my head. I slip into the stream, focusing only on the dim energy in the center to aim and thrust Cal dead center into the black hole.

Cal omits the blowback caused by stronger energy extinguishing a smaller one. Seeing a white light, I feel the force of the explosion, sending me flying backward, and then hitting the ground hard with the back of my head. Lights out.

CHAPTER 15

WATER, WATER FUCKING EVERYWHERE...

"Mmmmm," I moan, slowly coming to awareness. I crack one eye open, bright light hitting my eye like a baseball bat, my head pounding in pain, immediately shutting it, trying to go back to unconsciousness.

"She's awake!" I hear Virgil say near me.

"Sera?" G's voice is filled with worry.

"Mmmmm," is I all I can say in response. *Need to go back under to heal.*

"Okay, baby girl. Rest," Virgil whispers to me. I let myself relax, drifting back into unconsciousness.

Waking the second time is nearly not as painful. My head still hurts, but more like a mild headache. I open my eyes, still bright as hell out. I sit up slowly, stretching and feeling my body for any broken bones or internal damage. Just achy muscles from absorbing the energy from the explosion and being sent flying to land on my ass, err, head. Looking around, the guys have made a small campsite on the beach where I stopped the black hole from eating the second circle of hell.

Two of my guys are sleeping on each side of me while Red is on the lookout.

"Red?" I say hoarsely. He turns around, relief flooding his features when he sees me conscious and sitting up without help. He quickly gets up and walks over to me, kneeling down in front of me, looking me up and down to quickly assess my physical condition.

Red suddenly grabs me by the shoulders, pulling me into his chest and holding me tight. "We almost lost you!" he tells me, the worry and pain reflecting in his voice. "If you ever do anything that crazy and stupid again without telling us, I will spank your ass so hard you won't be able to walk for a week," Red firmly says, sounding extremely upset and pissed at me. *Damn.*

"I'm sorry," I say. "It was the only thing I can think of fast enough to call Lucifer's bluff. At least it worked," I say with a hint of optimism in my voice.

Red just growls. "I don't know what I am going to do with you, Sera," Red says in frustration.

"We should tie her up until she learns that being suicidal is not part of this mission," G says.

I gently pull away from Red and turn my body to G. *He looks like he hasn't slept in days!*

"Because he hasn't, Sera," Virgil states on the other side of me. "He was up for three whole days until he felt that you were out of danger of dying."

My guilt of putting undue stress on the guys is really weighing down on me.

"I'm sorry, guys," I state quietly. "I'm not used to relying on others in life or death situations. I'm used to seeing a problem and immediately acting to find a solution." I slide gingerly over to G, wrapping my arms around his chest and placing my head near his heart. I breathe in deeply, taking his scent in, smelling like a spicy aroma from an exotic middle eastern location. "I'm so sorry, G. I never would have done it if I thought it would worry you. All of you," I say sincerely, turning to Virgil and

Red as well. I go back to hugging G, feeling Virgil and Red close in behind me, all three hugging me at the same time.

We slowly break the group hug. "What now?" I ask.

"We are on a desert island, with no boat, surrounded by water. I've got no ideas," says Virgil.

"Me too," say Red and G. I get up, walking toward the water.

Something has been bothering me about this ocean. There are no waves, and no sounds of water moving along the shore. It's too perfect to be real.

I step into what I think is the water, but it's actually more sand. I sigh in irritation, looking back at the guys. "Lucifer painted an ocean mirage on the sand," I inform them. "Making us think we are stuck on a desert island. Lucifer really needs to get a fucking life and find a new hobby."

I start feeling out like I did in the first circle, looking for the archangel and door energy signatures. I have to really stretch my search out until I find both signatures that feel very far away.

Walking back to the guys, I say, "We need to go that way," pointing at the distant horizon. "Virgil, please get the tape, so we don't wander in circles as we did in the First Circle," I politely ask, giving him a kiss on the lips to show my appreciation. Virgil gives me a smile and goes into his bag to dig out the duct tape.

Just like in the First Circle, Virgil unrolls the tape about two feet, letting the roll hang on the bottom, handing the tail of the tape to me. Virgil waits for the roll to stop swinging, lowers himself to the ground to determine the tilt of the land, and points at the opposite direction of where I felt the energy signatures. "The tilt is much more prominent in this circle," Virgil states.

"Lucifer loves a good mind fuck, creating illusions that others would deem impossible," Red says. "Like creating this circle to look flat, making it look like it's all ocean, knowing that Sera can locate the archangel and door, and placing both on the opposite side of how this circle really tilts."

"Red," I say, "Lucifer will assume that we will walk directly towards the energy signatures, not away. But if we do that, we will be walking forever because all he did was create an illusion by bending a big fucking hill. No matter how you bend a hill, you can never connect the top to the bottom. Because then the laws of gravity would not exist. We will head down the hill as soon as we are all sufficiently rested," I say confidently to the group.

I walk to my pack, kneeling in the sand and opening the front pouch to grab a few protein bars and a bottle of water. I eat many protein bars since I've missed a few meals in the last three days and sparingly sip from my bottle of water.

My headache slowly clears. "I can do the first watch," I tell the guys. "All three of you have been worried sick about me for the last three days, so please rest." Nodding in agreement Virgil, G, and Red slip into their sleeping bags. Just didn't have the time to assess the temperature when we landed.

During my long watch, I practice the fire element. Creating different size fireballs and creating dancing figures in the fire. I even create a fire tornado, using air magic at the same time. I keep the fires small, so I can easily extinguish them if I get too tired.

I must have been at it for hours when I hear someone sucking in a sharp breath behind me. I'm in the middle of controlling a small fire tornado, about a foot in height when I lose my concentration, causing the fire tornado to vaporize into smoke. I turn my head and see Red sitting up in his sleeping bag, staring at me.

I walk over to Red, sitting next to him. "Red, why are you always shocked by my abilities?" I ask him pointblank.

"There's a prophecy," Red states. "There will be an angel that will not be created like the other angels. It will be born instead of made and will become the most powerful in existence. More powerful than Lucifer. Almost as powerful as the Creator." Red keeps going. "There are two prophecies concerning this angel, depending on the choices it makes. It will either bring life or death."

The way he says "death" gives me goosebumps. "Red, we are not talking about the apocalyptic kind of death, right?"

"More like the end of the universe kind of death," Red says calmly.

No one mentioned a doomsday prophecy!

"Wait? Were you made? How?"

He shrugs his shoulders. "No angel knows how they were made. All I know is that Lucifer was the first angel that was made."

"What does my abilities and hearing Cal have to do with the prophecy?"

"Only the Creator can control all the elemental magic. The Fire element belongs exclusively to Lucifer. Seeing that you have the affinities for three elements already, I can safely assume that you're the angel in the prophecy."

Not going to consider it right now. My next big question: "What the hell is the bet between the Creator and Lucifer?"

Red sighs, rubbing his hand through his blond hair. "Wish I fucking knew. It seems that Virgil and G don't know either. All we know is that you were sent to collect us." "Sera," Red says, going into command mode. "Go get some rest. We need you strong."

I sigh and quickly turn to him to give him a kiss on the cheek. "Night," I tell him.

He grabs my arms, pulling me forward, crushing my lips with his. I meet his tongue with mine, kissing him passionately in return. We gently break the kiss, those red eyes of his moving like molten lava. "Good night," he whispers huskily.

If we weren't about to embark on a dangerous trek, I would jump into his sleeping bag and have him fuck my brains out!

Standing up, I walk over to my pack, grabbing an eye mask, and slide into my sleeping bag. I place the cover on my eyes, blocking out any light. Lucifer wants us to go crazy with constant daylight. *He can go fuck himself!*

I immediately pass out.

CHAPTER 16

AND NOT A FUCKING DROP TO DRINK

Getting up a few hours later, we pack our gear and start heading in the opposite direction of the energies. Unlike Lust Land, where there is only one place that the sinners are eternally punished, we come upon many souls scattered, looking tattered and wasted like Tom Hanks in Castaway, either walking or crawling, all over the ocean-looking landscape.

Except, it seems that the water illusion is only meant for us, because we will desire water in this desolate country. The souls we encounter see just the illusion of what they overindulged in life. For some it was food, but mostly it was the addiction to drugs and alcohol.

The souls would drink and eat the sand thinking it was the substance they'd abused. Snort it up their noses, tear open their arms to "shoot up" with sand. All we hear is their own pitifully agonizing screams; not one of them seeming to hear the pain of their fellow sinners surrounding them. Not one of them offered solace or comfort to their fellow human.

"They were selfish in their gluttony in life by ignoring the pain that they caused others. Only caring about their pleasure," Virgil says. "Now they get to suffer in the misery they caused, never to get that pleasure they continue to seek out. For eternity."

I pity those souls, but they made their decisions in life. A thought comes to me. "What about those who were forced onto drugs, becoming dependent on them? Like girls forced into prostitution or drug babies?" I ask Virgil.

"This circle is for those who knew what would happen if they got addicted but still freely chose to destroy themselves. It's always about free will and knowing right from wrong," Virgil answers.

I nod in understanding.

We keep walking and walking, checking that the energy signature is behind us, stopping once in a while to use the duct tape; ensuring that we are still walking "downhill." Eventually, the energy signature is going to be in front of us since we are walking around a "small" world.

I'm grateful that Red put me through the hardest physical training in my life or else we would be stopping to rest much more often. The further we walk, the colder it gets. The colder it gets, the more energy we have to expend to keep warm. And to make the situation even worse, no fucking water!

It feels like we have been walking for days, always daylight, forcing us to ration our water supply to last for a couple more days. Even though we are tough to kill, we can still get stuck in this circle forever, not having the physical energy to move. Nothing eventful happens on our journey, making me wonder what's in store for us at the door.

Finally, I feel the energy in front of us, and we are probably halfway through our water. At our next stop, I inform the guys. They look terrible, still fucking handsome but worse than they usually look. I probably look the same. Their lips are chapped from lack of water, skin sallow and sunken in, eyes dull. My news doesn't have the moralizing effect that I hope it would bring.

Going first to Virgil, I kiss him on the lips, imparting a little of my energy to him. I step back, noticing an immediate difference. His face has some color, his skin not as cracked. I do the same for Red and G. Feeling a little dizzy, I lie down to rest for a bit, closing my eyes.

I am at rest. And I'm jolted awake. Red is running and carrying me in his arms. Terror and panic are on his face. I see Virgil and G keeping pace. Looking behind me, I see a black dust cloud heading our way, moving fast. "Is that a sandstorm?" I ask Red, with some concern in my voice.

"No! Fucking Fae!" he answers with a panicked voice.

"Fae? As in fairies?" I say with disbelief.

"Those little fuckers are the epitome of gluttony. They devour anything, including themselves if they cannot find food," G says.

Estimating our speed and how fast the Fae are chasing us, they will catch us within minutes. Looking up at Red, seeing that he's expending too much energy, I turn back to the black cloud barreling down on us.

Just like I practiced when we first got to this circle, I conjure up fire and wind, creating a fire tornado. Except, instead of using a tiny amount of energy to make a small tornado, I call for a lot of energy to create a massive fire tornado; a fire tornado that could be easily classified as an F4; maybe stretching to an F5. It could easily blow away a house within moments. In less than thirty seconds, the little fuckers don't stand a chance.

Feeling my energy at the breaking point, I stop. What was once a massive swarm of hungry little fairies that created a dense black cloud, is now barely fog. The survivors stop chasing us, dropping to the ground to eat the charcoal remains of their brethren.

"Red, please slow down," I tell him. "The Fae have stopped chasing us." He looks down at me like I lost my fucking mind. But Red turns his head slightly, having to see for himself. Seeing no more cloud, Red immediately slows down, then stops.

"What did you do, Sera?" Red asks with frustration in his voice.

Smiling innocently, I look him straight in the eye, saying "I made kindling for Lucifer's fireplace." Red dumps me to the ground. *Ouch!*

"What the fuck was that for?!" I yell up at him, rubbing my ass and back. Trying to get the stinging sensation to stop.

"I told you to stop taking risks without informing us!" Red yells at me.

Are you kidding me?! I stand up, pissed off for not at least getting a thank you for saving us. Again! I brush the dirt off my leather pants and then walk towards Red, stopping one inch away from Red's pissed off face. "Listen, asshole," my voice deadly quiet. "If you haven't noticed, my nose is not bleeding, and I didn't pass out from expending too much energy. So instead of treating me like a baby, you should be treating me like your equal. Because I just saved your ass. Again. And you have yet to thank me!"

I spin on my heal, heading over to Virgil, who carried my pack when I was being carried by Red. I grab my backpack from him, slinging it onto my back, giving Virgil a kiss on the cheek, saying, "Thank you." I turn back to Red. "See what I just did there, Red? I said, 'Thank you' to Virgil because he did something nice for me." With that, I turn away from Red and look to G to see how he's taking in the situation. G's expression is one of amusement, his grin getting wider.

Okay?

"Oof!" I groan out, my world twisting and going upside down. I realize that Red has grabbed and tossed me over his shoulder when I see his ass a foot down from my face. "Let me down!" I scream.

Red keeps marching forward, telling G and Virgil, "Be right back after I'm done disciplining her," he states, his tone set with finality.

"The fuck you will!" I yell into Red's back. *He's getting punched in the dick once I'm free!*

I hear Virgil snorting and choking. Then he's coughing so he can stop himself from laughing out loud. I just roll my eyes at Red's back. He carries me for a good ten minutes before he unceremoniously dumps me to the ground. Landing on my ass for the second time within thirty minutes makes me blow a fuse.

I slip into the stream, kicking Red's legs out from underneath him. Red lands on his back, using the momentum to roll backward, then uses his upper body strength to flip to his feet. He gives me a wicked grin. "My turn," he growls.

Slipping back into the stream, I try going ludicrous speed, but Red has me by the waist, causing me to slip out of the stream. Before I can say anything, Red's already kneeling, with me over his knee, spanking my ass, hard. I bite my inner cheek, preventing me from making any noise, but I couldn't stop the tears streaming down my face, feeling humiliated from being chastised.

He spanked me a few more times before releasing me. I was now a ball of fury and emotionally hurt. A nasty combination. "Now I know why Circe left you!" I hiss at him, my whole body shaking with rage. "She didn't want to get stuck with someone who still thinks that humans are inferior. If I had a choice, I'd leave your ass too!" And with that, I find any energy I have left in me, slip into the stream, and go beyond ludicrous speed; heading in a random direction.

"Sera!" I hear Red yell.

Fuck off!

I am in the stream until my nose starts bleeding and I'm exhausted. I slip out of the stream, stopping, dropping my pack and curling next to it. I don't care if I don't ever see the guys again. They don't consider me their equal. They knew Red was going to punish me but no one stopped him!

I pass out, letting my emotional pain and anger dissipate. I don't know how long I sleep, but I don't care. I would wake up, take a sip of water, then pass back out. When I finally wake up, I feel emotionally empty. Nothing matters anymore. I ignore the pull in my chest. Probably my bonds with the guys. I focus on the door energy.

Taking another sip of water, I pick up my pack and start walking towards the energy. I don't even feel his presence until he stops right in front of me. "Get out of my way Uriel," I demand, reverting back to Red's Archangel's name because I'm pissed. Avoiding any eye contact, I try to step around him, but he grabs my arm, stopping me.

Creating fire in my other hand, I place it on top of Red's hand that has me by the arm, singeing his hand. He immediately releases me with a surprised yelp. "Don't ever fucking touch me!" I snarl and start walking away from him.

"Sera!" It was Red's voice, but it sounded more like a sob than a command. I turn around feeling confused. He's on his knees, his head bowed.

"What, Uriel?" I demand. He looks up at me, his face full of pain and remorse.

The area around his eyes is red like he's been crying. "You were right. I'm sorry I humiliated you like that. I keep forgetting how strong and independent you are, and it scares the shit out of me. I'm so afraid of losing you, that I became an overbearing asshole." His voice sounds down and sad.

"I don't know what to say, Red. I thought I earned your trust, but you never took the time to earn mine. You and G are both egotistical, a major character flaw for an angel. I now just want to get out of here," I say with a sigh. I'm too dead inside to say anything more.

Red looks up at me, pleadingly. "I'm so sorry, Sera. Please forgive me."

I just stand there, numb to the core. "Why?" I ask him.

"Because..." he mutters.

"Because why, Red?" I still demand.

"Because I am yours as you are mine. Equally," he says.

"And?" I keep pushing.

"And," Red sighs, "because I love you as much as you love us."

My heart flutters in my chest. *Red loves me?!*

Tears start spilling out the sides of my eyes. Red stands up and slowly walks towards me. When he's less than a foot away, he opens his arms. *Call me an idiot, but I love the asshole.*

I run into his arms, letting him hold me. He kisses the top of my head, keeping me tight, while I press my head against his chest. I breathe in his gingerbread scent. Red feels and smells like home to me. I move my head away from his chest and I look up at him, seeing love reflecting in his eyes. Red lowers his head and gently kisses me.

I tentatively kiss him back, becoming bolder each second. That was all that was needed to start the fire within me. My kisses are becoming more aggressive, trying to tell him that I need him now! He understands my need, matching it with his own because he starts kissing me fervently.

Red gently lifts me up and lowers me to the ground, placing his body between my legs. Our kissing becomes passionate, our tongues dancing, igniting a fire between my legs.

I break our kiss, pleadingly say, "I want you inside me."

Smiling down at me, Red sits up and starts peeling off my boots. I pull my leather pants and underwear down to my knees, letting Red take them off the rest of the way. The cold air hits my legs, giving me goosebumps.

Red unbuttons his pants, pulling them down from his hips, his massive cock springing out. Red leans forward, sliding his warm body back over mine. The head of his cock is at my wet and ready entrance.

Red slowly pushes himself into me, taking his sweet time to fill me. Finally sheathing himself all the way to the hilt, Red starts slowly rocking into me, staring into my eyes. He makes slow love to me, taking his time to build the sweet pleasure that is about to break, while never breaking eye contact.

When I'm about to burst, my eyes start to flutter. "Don't close your eyes, Sera," Red growls. "I want to see your eyes when you come for me." That statement sets me off. The orgasm is strong, long, and fucking intense. I don't close my eyes, instead letting them glaze over, shouting my pleasure. At the same time, Red comes deep within me, crying my name over and over in pure ecstasy.

My eyes refocus, looking at Red's beautiful face. He thrusts a few more times before laying his body entirely onto me, kissing my neck, my face, and lips. Raising his head above mine, he says calmly, "God you drive me to insanity."

"Guess it must be love then," I tease.

"I love you, Sera," Red says seriously.

"I love you too," I tell him in return.

After cleaning ourselves and getting dressed, we put on our packs and start walking towards the energy signatures. "What about Virgil and G," I ask Red.

"I told them I fucked things up with you and will go find you. To beg for your forgiveness," he adds. "They said that they will meet us at the location of the energies. Virgil will use the tape trick to ensure that they are still walking downhill."

I just nod my head.

We keep walking and walking. Stopping for short rests and water sips. It's getting colder and colder but not cold enough to see my breath.

I feel the energy signatures of the Archangel and door getting closer and closer. I also start feeling Virgil and G's distinct signatures as well. Coming closer from the opposite direction.

Red and I keep walking in long silences, conserving our energy. Our water supply is running dangerously low. In the distance, I start seeing small hills. The more miles we walk, the hills go from small to mountain size. Keeping a steady pace and intermittent rest stops, it feels like a couple more days until we are at the bottom of a rock staircase, climbing up the most extensive mountain I've ever seen. We have a little water left.

G and Virgil's presences are incredibly close. We wait, seeing them walking towards us out on the horizon. When they get to us, I walk up to them, noting the dark scowls on their faces. If I weren't dehydrated, I'd be crying for acting foolish. "I'm sorry," I tell them, stopping right in front of them. Feeling ashamed, I look down at the ground.

"Why did you run away from us?" G asks me in an angry tone.

"You didn't stop Red from taking me to get disciplined. I felt that you both didn't consider me your equal and you have no trust in me or my judgment. I didn't feel part of the team. Why should I stay?" I confess quietly, still looking at the ground. I hear a frustrated sigh. I look up, both men's face is a little softer, but G still has that troubled look in his eyes.

"I truly am sorry that I ran," I repeat, looking at both G and Virgil. "Please forgive me?"

Virgil sighs, rubbing his hand over his face. "Sera, you scared the shit out of us. When we couldn't feel you close, and I couldn't hear your thoughts, we went crazy with fear. When Red told us what had happened between you two, it was G who had to pull me off of him. I would never have let Red take you if I knew he was going to follow through on his threat."

I nod my head, feeling ashamed for not trusting Virgil.

Looking at G, he's looking back at me, still with a troubled look on his face. "I knew Red would discipline you. Being created as an archangel and a general to lead armies and living as Red and I have, we are not used to someone making command decisions for us. Red and I will have to get used to others leading," he says, sounding resigned that he cannot control me. But there is still a troubled look in his expression.

"What is it, G?" I ask him politely. I have a sense that he wants to tell me something but is hesitant.

"Nothing, I'm just tired from worrying that something awful had happened to you," G says. I know he's not telling me the truth, but I drop the subject.

"Let's make camp and rest," I suggest. "We don't know what's waiting for us up at the top of those stairs."

CHAPTER 17

How To Wag the Dog

We consolidate our water supply, each of us taking sips. Looking up the stairs, I cannot even see where the stairs end. *Where's a fucking elevator when you need one?*

I look at Virgil, knowing he's still upset with me because he's ignoring my stare. But I catch a little crack of a grin on the side of his mouth, knowing that he can still hear my thoughts. *I love him when he laughs at my vulgarity!*

Oops. Virgil snaps his head up, eyes on me. I look down, feeling my whole body flush in embarrassment. I didn't mean for the "L" word to slip. I hear Virgil getting up, walking over to where I'm sitting and sits right next to me. His body touching mine.

Virgil gently grabs and lifts my chin towards him, making me stare into those breathtaking, silver swirling eyes. He raises one of his brown eyebrows, giving me a questioning look.

I inwardly roll my eyes. 'Yes, damnit! I love you!'

Virgil releases my chin, giving me a big grin. He leans forward, his mouth right next to my ear, whispering, "I love you too." A wave of relief and happiness floods my chest. I let out a shaky breath, not realizing that I was holding it in. Virgil gives me a sweet kiss on the lips.

I lean my head against his shoulder. *Love is so tiring!*

I hear a chuckle emanating from Virgil's chest. 'Tell me about it!' I hear Virgil's voice say in my head. I immediately lift my head, looking at him quizzically.

"What's the matter, Sera?"

"I just heard your thoughts," I tell him.

'No fucking way!' Virgil says in my head.

'Yes fucking way,' I think back. Now it's Virgil's turn to look quizzically at me. The expression on his face is priceless! *Wish I had a camera!*

"What? Why?" Virgil says out loud.

'The look you're giving me is hilarious!' I think, starting to laugh. Ever laugh so hard until tears are coming out at something that's should only be considered amusing? That's me right now. Laughing hysterically, tears streaming out, in the Second Circle of Hell.

G and Red are staring at me like I finally I'm having a mental breakdown. Their expressions only fuel my laughter until my sides hurt. I need a good laugh. I cannot even remember the last time I laughed that hard. When I stop laughing, I feel so much better. Looking at Virgil, who's smiling back at me, I think, 'Thank you. I needed that!'

Virgil's smile widens. 'Anytime, baby! You have a beautiful laugh,' I hear him say. I snort in response.

"Are we missing something?" G asks. I look over to him and Red. G's frowning, wondering what the hell is going on. Red, on the other hand, just smiles at me, giving me a wink. I give Red a big smile. *It's nice to be loved and understood.*

But I feel a little sadness. G still doesn't understand me.

After each of us gets a chance to sleep and recover, we start climbing the stairway to take us deeper into Hell. The higher we go, the colder it gets. That would make complete sense if we were on earth. But we are in Hell, being played on a chessboard by the very first master of deception.

"I believe we are descending," I say to no one in particular. My ass, thighs, and calf muscles aren't burning like they should from climbing upstairs for hours. I cannot even see the ground when I look behind me. Meaning that just like the rest of the circle, the landscape curves.

And we keep on going up. I mean down. What feels like a whole day later, we arrive at a cave entrance going into the mountain. All around the opening there are "Beware of Floppsy, Moppsy, and Cotton Tail" signs in what seems to be every single language imaginable. There is even a sign in Braille. *That's so wrong!*

Suddenly there is a massive roar, causing the ground to shake so hard I fall on my ass. And out comes Floppsy, Moppsy, and Cotton Tail! A giant three-headed dog the size of a fucking double-decker bus! Its fur black, the eyes, all six, gleaming gold.

Barreling down on me, FMC (my new nickname for them if I live!) cause me to panic, freezing me in fear. The only thing I can do is sit and watch my death coming at me, yapping and snarling those razor-sharp teeth times three.

FMC suddenly stops no more than a foot away from me. It starts sniffing the air with its three noses. Then it walks closer to me. The middle head starts smelling my boots, then my leather pants and keeps going up all the way to my hair.

And then I'm pinned down, being covered by a substantial wet tongue. Saliva and drool running down my face. *Gross!*

Wait! Where the fuck are the guys? Sitting up, pushing the nose on one of FMC's heads away from me. "Good puppy!" I say with false bravado. "Back up! That's it! Back up!" FMC back's up about five feet away from me, ears perked, three tongues sticking out, tail wagging. "Sit!" I command. FMC obeys. *Cool!*

Turning my head to the left and right, the guys are still on the ground, eyes open, not moving. Like they are still petrified. 'Virgil, what's going on?' I think.

'If you look at that thing in one of their eyes, you will stay frozen in fear,' is Virgil's response.

I turn back to FMC. "Please release my mates," I say with authority. FMC huffs like I'm taking its toys away. "Now," I command. FMC growls. "I'll rub your ears," I say, resorting to bribery. That works!

I hear breaths releasing and bodies moving. "Good boy!" I say.

FMC's three heads growl at me again. I walk a little to the side to see up FMC's so called "skirt". "Oh! Sorry! I mean good girl!"

FMC lays down, wanting me to fulfill my end of the bargain. I walk over to one of the outer heads and start scratching her enormous ears.

Must have taken me over an hour to scratch each and every ear thoroughly.

Completing the last ear, FMC stands up and the head of the ear I just finished scratching gives me a nuzzle and a lick. Up my whole body. *Definitely going to need a shower and new clothes.*

The guys have given FMC and me wide berth during the ear scratching session. "Ready to go?" I ask, acting like getting a ginormous dog with three heads for a pet is the most normal thing in the world. Or in Hell.

I start walking towards the entrance, FMC walking by my side, the guys a few feet behind us. 'Seriously?' I think to Virgil. 'You're afraid?'

'That's a deadly beast. I feel safer back here away from the teeth,' is his reply.

'Pray she doesn't have gas!' I tease.

'How do you know it's a "she?"'

'I checked the old fashion way.'

I reach my hand out, patting FMC. Her fur is incredibly soft! She makes a grunting sound in her chest. *My puppy likes that?*

'Sera! You know that's a fucking Hellhound right?' Virgil admonishes me in my head. 'And that's not just any Hellhound, that's Lucifer's primary Hellhound.'

I shrug my shoulders, still petting FMC. 'She's mine now,' I tell Virgil firmly. 'And I feel a connection with her.' No response from Virgil.

We walk through the entrance of the cave into total darkness, feeling that we are very close to the energy signatures. I let FMC take the lead. This is her home after all. We keep on walking in the dark. I feel the rough surface of the cave floor through my boots. I keep holding onto FMC, the guys following us.

It was a few more minutes until I feel the change in the floor texture. Instead of a rough surface, the floor is smooth. If I had to guess, I would say the floor is marble. The darkness is giving way to light.

The lighting shows me beautiful white Italian marble on the floor, extending to the walls, turning to columns. I feel like I am walking in a documentary of the Vatican. As I keep on walking, the cave opens into a massive, opulent foyer, leading to a marble column banister.

Arriving at the railing, I take in the room's decor. There are twin staircases in white marble, curving down to another level that is entirely in black marble. I look up, and there is a gigantic crystal chandelier; something that could have come out of a Victorian mansion.

It's also a bit cold in here. Having nowhere else to go but down, I walk down one of the twin staircases, FMC still beside me. When I step onto the black marble floor, there's a massive roar that shakes the room. FMC actually whines from all three mouths, places her ears back, and tucks in her tail.

"Whatever made that roar has that Hellhound really fucking scared," states G.

I nod my head in agreement, swallowing loudly.

I start feeling for the energy signatures, noting that one of them is near and on the move. "There is an archangel nearby," I say. I retrieve Cal.

"Ready?" I ask. Cal does not respond but starts to glow a golden color.

Looking around the bottom level foyer, I notice a lot of doors lining the walls. But I'm only looking for one. *I wonder what's behind the red door?*

"You have to reference an old porn movie while we are on the hunt?" Virgil asks me out loud.

I turn my head towards him, cracking a smile, "How did you know what I was referencing?"

"I've been on Earth for more than the one day you've met me on," Virgil grins back.

I send him a kiss. I have to be me.

Walking over to the large, red double doors, I touch the ornate handle with my free hand. No fortune cookie saying appears on the door. *Thank God!*

Turning the knob, I push the door open, revealing a vast corridor in blood red marble. I open the other door so FMC can come with us.

Walking down the red corridor is a bit unnerving. Hard not to compare the shiny red marble to fresh blood. But that's probably what Lucifer had in mind. I feel the moving energy signature coming our way.

FMC pauses, lowering her ears back, growling from deep in her throat; the fur on her back rising. I stop with her. Her senses times three are far more superior than mine. I don't need to say anything to the guys, after they witness FMC's reaction.

The second roar is ear-splitting. I have to cover my ears to prevent my eardrums from bursting. Whatever it is, it's heading straight down the corridor, doing Mach One.

Seeing into the stream, there is a huge wolf-like animal, running on all fours, with golden, glowing eyes. FMC slips into the stream before I can stop her, meeting wolf-thing halfway. FMC is much bigger, but the wolf-thing is a thousand time more agile and powerful. It also seems that the wolf-thing's claws are razor sharp.

The sound of the two wolves fighting is heartbreaking. I hear FMC scream in pain as the wolf-thing tears into her. "I'm going to help FMC!" I yell at the guys, my tone brokering no arguments.

I slip into the stream, going as fast as I can, my chest squeezing every time FMC screams in pain. By the time I get to the fight, I'm pissed. *No one hurts my dog!*

Wolf-thing nearly misses my presence. But it is enough for me to sink Cal through its back, slicing through to the front. At the same time, the fucker claws my arm.

Falling to the ground, I'm screaming in agony, an unholy fire running up my arm through my body. *Fucker's claws are poisonous!* I'm thrashing everywhere, the pain unimaginable. I never wanted to die so much in my life as I do now. The worst part is that I'm coherent the whole time, the poison not letting me drift off into oblivion.

"Sera!" I don't know who bellowed my name, but all three of my mates' faces are suddenly in front of me. My screams and tears must be unnerving them because they look so lost and helpless.

"Cal!" I scream to them.

Red turns, disappearing from my sight, returning an instant later. He places Cal on the wound. "Little one," Cal says calmly in my head while I'm still screaming in pain, "I need to draw this poison out. The pain is going to be more intense than what you are feeling now. Forgive me, but there is no other way."

"Do it!" I scream in my head.

Cal has never been wrong since I first heard the voice and he's definitely not wrong now. The fire I was feeling, turns into a fucking inferno! I scream and cry while G and Virgil hold me down to keep me from thrashing while Red keeps Cal on the wound.

Time slows when you're in a world of pain. The worse the pain is, the slower time goes. My pain feels like it lasts for years, not minutes. My voice goes hoarse from screaming for so long. When the last drop of poison is out of me, that's when I finally pass out.

Opening my eyes, I feel like I've been run over by a steamroller. My body hurts everywhere. When I am able to focus, I take in the plaster ceiling with crown molding around a small chandelier. Then I feel blankets on top of me. I move my aching arms to push the sheets off me, the cold air hitting my skin instantly makes me realize that I'm naked. *Like the guys haven't seen me naked before.*

Pushing the blankets off and gently sitting up, I look around the room. Unlike the tacky red and gold room I stayed in during my visit in the first circle of Hell, this room has soft blue and grey color tones. The room seems like a nice place for relaxation.

I hear snoring near me. I look around, seeing that I'm in a huge bed that can easily fit five people. But I'm alone in the bed. I slowly move to the side of the bed that the snoring is coming from.

At the edge of the bed, I look down and see FMC on the floor, curled up, all three of her heads asleep. I'm relieved that she survived wolf-thing's poisonous claws, and I am forever grateful that she protected us.

I feel out for my guys. I feel a fourth energy signature with them. "Good morning, Virgil! I'm awake!" I think to him. Our bond has grown even stronger since we admitted our love to each other, letting us talk telepathically.

I feel a presence coming swiftly towards me. Definitely not Virgil since he cannot slip into the stream. Instead, it is Red appearing next to the bed. He gives my naked body a slow perusal. "Did you call?" he asks.

What?!

"I felt that you were awake and calling out," Red explains.

"I thought only Virgil can hear my thoughts?"

"Our bond must be getting stronger," he tells me, giving me a smile that reaches those beautiful red eyes. So handsome! Red's smile gets wider, showing me his perfect teeth. *Shit! Now I have to watch my thoughts around two men.*

Virgil and G walk into the room. Virgil smiles at me. I don't need to hear his thoughts to know that he is relieved that I'm okay. I look at G and his expression tells me one thing, but his eyes are saying something different. G's looks "happy" that I'm awake, but his eyes are troubled. *What's wrong with him?*

Out from behind Virgil and G steps the fourth energy signature I felt. I quickly grab a sheet to cover myself. This angel has golden eyes; swirling pools of pure gold. *Why are angels incredibly beautiful?*

His skin is a dark bronze, reminding me of someone who might originate from the North African region. His hair is a shocking white color. His face sculpted like one of the ancient pharaoh statues, long and elegant with high cheekbones. His body is also shaped like one of the Egyptian figures I have seen on Egyptian documentaries. Long, lean, and muscular.

Of course, like an ancient Egyptian, the archangel is wearing a soft brown tunic and kilt. Golden arm bracelets wrap around his strong biceps and golden sandals cover his feet. *Surprised he's not cold.*

"Sera, this is Raphael," Red informs me. "He is the archangel of Temperance." Raphael gives Red a sharp look. "Raphael wants to know if it was you who stabbed him with the sword?" Red says to me apologetically, knowing that I'm not going to take any angel chauvinist bullshit.

Looking straight at Raph, my new nickname for him, I prissily say

"Why yes, Raph! It was me who got the drop on you while you were trying to maul my dog to death, stabbing you with Cal. Why?"

Raph doesn't even bother to look at me, eyes still on Red, telling Red, "She needs to be disciplined and learn some manners. She doesn't understand who her betters are."

I roll my eyes. *My betters?*

Red keeps looking at me, cracking a small smile. I look at Virgil, and he's smiling at me also. Lastly, I look at G, face down, the expression is serious. I huff in exasperation. At least the ones who say they love me, support me. Which gives me the courage for what I am about to do next.

"Oh, Raph?" I say sweetly, letting the sarcasm drip into my tone. "The day I recognize you as my better is the day the Ninth Circle of Hell becomes a hotspot for a tropical vacation. When you recognize me as your equal is when I will allow you into my presence. Until then… Fuck. Off."

Raph finally looks at me, and he is fucking pissed. His eyes are glowing a brighter gold, his bronze skin darkening. I yawn. *Got more important issues to deal with.*

Tapping into my power, I call up the wind to lift Raph like a feather and blow him out my door. The shock of my air power and the swiftness in which I am able to kick him out of my room prevents Raph from making any noise of protest. *Now to the real problem.*

"Virgil. Red.I need to talk to G alone," I politely tell them. Virgil and Red immediately turn around and walk out the doorway, closing the door. "Straighten Raph's ass out while you both are out there!" I think to Red and Virgil.

Turning to G, I say, "What is it? Ever since we came to this circle you've been distant. What's wrong?" I can see G is extremely uncomfortable with my line of questioning. But I'm a patient person. *Sometimes.*

G stands in front of the bed, head down, not looking at me with his green eyes. I drop the sheet and silently slide across the bed and gently touch his cheek. He startles, swatting my hand away. *What?*

Looking down at the bed covers, taking a moment to regain my composure, I look back up at G. He now looks angry. *For touching him?*

I take a deep breath, remaining calm, even though I want to break down and cry. "Okay G," my voice as calm and cold as ice. "I thought we had come to terms on the boat, but it seems that I'm wrong. Like I told you back then. I will not force you to be one of my mates. If you want, I will attempt to break the bond again."

G runs his hand through his hair, frustration emanating from every movement he's making. "I don't know what I want anymore, Sera," he honestly tells me.

"What's changed, G?" I ask.

"You promised to treat us equally, but I'm starting to feel left out," he mumbles.

Huh? "G, please come here," I quietly command. He reluctantly walks over to the bed. "When have I not treated you as an equal?" G shrugs his shoulders, not bothering to look up at me. There's something else going on.

"I'm going to touch you?" I politely ask. G nods his head in agreement. I sit up on my knees, again gently touching his cheek. He closes his eyes like I'm causing him pain. I move my face towards his, gently kissing his lips.

G groans, slightly hesitating, before pulling me into his body. He's desperately kissing me as if he's afraid of something. I wish he would tell me what's really bothering him.

Our kiss becomes hot with need. Our tongues are fighting and tangling around each other. I'm already naked, so I start pulling on G's shirt. He raises both arms, grabbing his shirt from behind his head, hurriedly pulling it off. He breaks our kiss to take off the rest of his clothes.

I shift my body back towards the center of the bed, lying down. G follows, crawling forward until his body is on top of mine, his hips nestled between my legs. I'm already wet for him when he shoves his massive cock into me.

I moan in pleasure, already moving in rhythm with his powerful thrusts. He's pounding hard into me. I keep myself from coming, wanting his rough lovemaking to last.

When I do come, I scream, the pleasure incredibly intense. So intense that my wings pop out. G also comes, feeling his hot liquid shooting deep within me. He must have liked it because his wings also popped out.

G collapses on top of me, both of us covered in sweat, breathing heavy. I gently touch his ebony wing, saying "I love you."

G snaps his head up, looking down at me in confusion. I shyly smile, reaching my hand out to touch his face. He smacks it away again. Crack! There goes my heart! The pain of G's rejection makes me numb all over. I can't feel anything now.

G's wings disappear as he quickly pulls out of me, moving to the edge of the bed to stand up. Bending over, he gathers his clothes and takes rapid strides towards the door. You would think the room is on fire by how fast he is moving. Doesn't look back at me when he flings the door open and marches out.

I don't know what I did to change G's mind about me. And I refuse to keep someone bonded to me just to use me for his pleasure. I should be strong enough to break the soul bond now.

"Sera! Don't!" Virgil shouts through my open doorway. I ignore Virgil's warning, too hurt and angry to care anymore. My heart is shattered. I quickly tap into my energy. Remember not having a diamond cutter the first time I tried severing the soul bond? I have a fucking nuke this time.

Breaking the bond is much easier and feels less taxing. I never realized how weak my bond with G truly was.

By the time Red and Virgil get to me, the bond is no more. The pain in my soul is excruciating; I've lost a piece of me. And I hate G for that. I've never hated anyone in my life. But I hate now. With new clarity and insight, I use the hate and anger to fuel the cold reasoning, to be dead inside, that is washing over me.

Instead of Red and Virgil finding me in a pool of tears, crying my heart out on the bed, they see me calm and collected. Sitting up, completely naked in all my glory, I feel a cold resolve with my decision in breaking the bond. I let that resolve make me peaceful enough for my wings to pop out. I turn my head to glance at a wing. Instead of them being fiery red, they are now a fiery black and blue.

Interesting.

Red and Virgil both look shocked to see my new wings.

Raph comes in next, a sword in his hand. "I feel Lucifer's presence. Where the fuck—" Raph starts asking, stopping mid-question when he sees me and my wings.

"We are in big fucking trouble," Red says out loud without saying why. Virgil doesn't respond, staring at me with sadness and sympathy.

"What is she, Uriel?" Raph demands.

"She's my mate," Red says proudly.

I shift my gaze to Virgil, wondering if he'll also leave me. He must have sensed my question. "She's my mate also," he states, resigned in knowing that he will have to take the good with the bad. Just like me.

To Be Continued...

Printed in the United States
By Bookmasters